Virginia Bound

Amy Butler

CLARION BOOKS * NEW YORK

Clarion Books
a Houghton Mifflin Company imprint
215 Park Avenue South, New York, NY 10003
Copyright © 2003 by Amy Butler

The text was set in 13.5-point Adobe Garamond.

www.houghtonmifflinbooks.com

Printed in the U.S.A.

Library of Congress Cataloging-in-Publication Data

Butler, Amy.
Virginia bound / by Amy Butler.
p. cm.
Summary: Thirteen-year-old orphaned beggar Rob Brackett is kidnapped
from the streets of London and taken to the New World for a cruel tobacco
farmer master, who also owns a Pamunkey Indian girl named Mattoume.
ISBN 0-618-24752-1 (alk. paper)
[1. Orphans—Fiction. 2. Indentured servants—Fiction. 3. Pamunkey
Indians—Fiction. 4. Indians of North America—Virginia—Fiction.
5. Virginia—History—Colonial period, ca. 1600-1775—Fiction.] I. Title.

PZ7.G8443 Vi 2003
[Fic]—dc21   2002008722

QUM 10 9 8 7 6 5 4 3 2

For David, who crossed the Atlantic, too

Chapter 1

Night was drawing in, a February evening with frost on its breath. As London fell into darkness, fingers of fog crept over the banks of the Thames. Soon the only light was candlelight, which flickered and danced in diamond-paned windows.

Beneath one of those windows, in a narrow alley not far from the docks, sat Rob Brackett, counting his money. He piled the coins atop one another, then spread them out in his hand. Two farthings and a battered ha'penny. A paltry sum, however you looked at it, in this year of our Lord, 1627—hardly enough to buy a bun loaf, let alone supper for two.

"Hope Nell had more luck," he muttered to himself.

But Nell was late, and that had him worried. He slipped the small coins into his ragged doublet. Perhaps he ought to go looking for her.

She was only nine, was Nell, and too trusting by

half. Rob minded the day he'd found her huddled in an alley, tears streaming down her grimy face. He'd tried to ignore her, of course. It was hard enough to look out for himself, without taking on a weepy young'un as well. But the sight of her had plagued him something terrible, and in the end he'd asked her what was wrong. Her aunt had died that morning, she told him, leaving her alone in the world. The next thing he knew, he was offering to look out for her until she learned to survive on her own.

She was a slow learner. Three months, now, he'd been saddled with her. Not that she'd been such a terrible trial, when all was said and done. In fact, he had to admit that sometimes he rather liked having her about.

Not worth the worry, though, he told himself. *Be good when she's gone.*

Scowling, he peered into the darkness. Where *was* she?

Footsteps pattered at the head of the alley. Rob rose warily to his feet. Was it Nell? Or was it a beggarman, searching for a place to sleep? Rob hoped not. Only thirteen, and small for his age, he was no match for a full-grown man. But at least he'd have surprise on his side. With his dark hair and sooty clothes, he'd be hard to spot till the very last second. He tensed his muscles, ready to spring.

A small girl came rushing toward him, flaxen hair gleaming in the faint light. Rob relaxed. It was Nell.

"Oh, Rob! They—"

"Hush!" Crouching low, he pointed to the window. "They'll hear."

Nell crept up to his side.

"What happened?" he asked.

"'Twas those rogues by St. Paul's. They caught me' on the way home and took all my money—three ha'pennies and seven farthings, the best I've ever done. And they tore my cloak, too!" Tears filled her eyes as she held up the tattered felt.

Rob hated to see her so upset. Awkwardly, he patted her back. "Never you mind, lass. Them ruffians by St. Paul's is a sneaky lot. There's plenty as run afoul of 'em."

"Did they ever steal from you?"

"O' course. They did for me lots o' times, back when I was first on the streets." That was over a year ago, but Rob remembered it clearly: the humiliation of begging, followed by the even greater humiliation of having the ruffians relieve him of his takings. "You learn to see 'em coming," he said now. "It just takes practice, that's all."

With a grubby fist, Nell tugged her cloak back into place. "I expect I need more practice, then." She smiled shakily at him and drew a deep breath.

"Best to breathe shallow," Rob advised.

He was too late. Nell made a face and clapped a hand over her nose. "Ugh!"

For the hundredth time Rob wished they'd found a place for themselves that wasn't so close to the Thames. Here they were so near the docks that the stench of the river was well-nigh unbearable. But he and Nell didn't have much choice as to lodgings. They were orphans, outcasts. This small alley—rife with rats and refuse but mercifully free of other occupants—was the best they'd been able to do.

"Seven farthings," Nell mourned, her hand still over her nose. "And three ha'pennies."

It was indeed a great loss, but to comfort her, Rob said, "'Tis only money, it is."

"But I . . ." Her hand muffled the last words.

"What's that?"

Nell took her hand away from her face. "I wanted to buy you a hammer."

A hammer. Rob's fingers tingled at the mere mention of the word. He'd been barely five years old when he'd sawed his first board in his father's shop, nine when he'd built his first bench. By eleven he'd learned how to carve a bunch of grapes so ripe and round, you'd put out your hand to pluck one.

His father had taken great pride in his progress. "Brackett & Son, that's who we'll be," he'd promised, "just as soon as you finish your apprenticeship."

But before Rob's apprenticeship could be arranged, a fire had burned down the shop, taking Rob's father along with it. In the space of a few hours, Rob had lost everything he'd ever hoped for, and everything he'd ever loved.

Nell twisted her apron uncertainly. "Mayhap you'd rather have a chisel?"

Rob did his best to keep his voice even. "'Tis no good me having tools, Nell, when I've no chance of practicing me trade. There's too many carpenters in London as it is."

She frowned at him. "You don't know that—"

"I do! What do you think I'm doing, all the time you're off to St. Paul's?" He didn't wait for her answer. "Looking for work, that's what. And no one will hire me. Times are hard, they say. They'll not take anyone on, let alone a boy who was never apprenticed."

"I didn't know you were looking for work," said Nell in a small voice. "I thought you were begging, like me."

Truth was, sometimes he did beg. The magistrates didn't like it, since he had no license, but how else was a boy to keep body and soul together? By stealing, perhaps—but stealing was a dangerous game. Though Rob wasn't above pilfering the odd apple or two, he drew the line at turning house robber or cutpurse. For crimes like that a boy could be whipped or hanged or sent as a servant to savage Virginia, three thousand miles away. Not that you had to be guilty to find yourself bound for Virginia. Bridewell, one of London's orphan houses, had sent hundreds of its charges there—which was why Rob and Nell were determined to stay well away from the place.

"I hate begging," Rob said now. "I hate the way people look at me like I was no better than the dirt on their shoes."

"That's why I wanted to buy a hammer." Nell sounded close to tears. "So you'd not have to beg anymore. And mayhap we'd find a family to take us in. . . ."

Rob gritted his teeth. Nell was always babbling about a family taking them in. Why she had such faith in the kindness of strangers he didn't know. Three months on London's streets ought to have knocked that foolishness out of her. But perhaps he had only himself to blame, for hadn't he shielded her from the worst of what those streets had to offer?

"And once we find a family," Nell continued, "you can practice your trade—"

"No decent family'd take in the likes of us."

"But—"

"How many times do I have to say it, Nell? 'Tis no use expecting someone to come to our rescue. And 'tis no use pretending people are kind, because they aren't. 'Tis every man for hisself in this world." He'd learned that quickly enough after his father had died.

"Look out for yourself, that's what I say. And don't trust no one."

Nell blinked. "I trust you."

Rob glanced down the dark alley, avoiding her wide-open eyes. "You'd do better not to," he mumbled. "Anyhow, like I told you, we're only together temporary like, till you can manage on your own."

"But I—"

Rob shook his head and rose to his feet. "We've gabbled long enough, Nell. 'Tis time we went to Tavern Row and bought ourselves some supper."

Nell brightened. "You've money, then?"

"Enough for a bit o' bread from the Bird in Hand. No more." He showed her his few coins, then tucked them back into their hideaway in the hem of his doublet.

He led Nell down the dark streets, keeping an eye out for trouble. As they wound their way to the waterfront, the dank smell of the river grew ever more pungent. At last they reached the head of Tavern Row, which was alive with river men and rough laughter. Crowds of careless strangers bumped into each other, swinging their arms and singing at the top of their lungs.

"Stick close, Nell," Rob warned, "and look sharp."

Together they pushed their way down the street. The air was heavy with the smells of good cooking: bread and meat and pies and puddings. But a body couldn't feast on smells alone. Rob wanted food in his mouth, in his belly. Even a bit of bread would be better than nothing.

The Bird in Hand was the smallest tavern in the row, and the cheapest. At the sight of it, Rob's head began to swim.

"Rob?"

Nell's voice seemed very distant. "I'm all right," he told her. He reached into his doublet for the coins. "I'm just hungry, that's—"

He stopped still. He couldn't feel the coins. Not a single one.

"What is it?" Nell asked.

Rob didn't answer. He felt for the coins again. Nothing.

"Rob?"

Rob shook his head. Perhaps the coins had fallen through the lining and gotten lost in the doublet's hem. If so, he ought to hear them clinking when he jiggled the garment. He shook it, flapping both sleeves. Not even the tiniest jingle.

He ran his fingers along the edge of the doublet. And there he found it: a hole in the hem, right where he'd hidden the coins. They must have worn straight through the threadbare garment.

Rob stared at the hole and then at Nell.

All their money was gone.

Chapter 2

"I ought to have heard them drop," said Rob for the
third time. "I ought to have heard summat."

He and Nell were standing outside the Bird in
Hand, some yards away from the crowds milling
around its door.

"'Twasn't your fault," said Nell. "'Tis hard to hear
anything at all on Tavern Row."

She spoke truly enough. All along the street men
were piping merry tunes on pennywhistles. Sailors
were clapping and singing. Stray dogs howled alongside them. No wonder Rob had missed the clink of
the coins as they fell.

All the same, he blamed himself for their misfortune. And misfortune it certainly was, for they'd never
find the coins again. Either passersby had picked
them up as soon as they'd fallen, or they'd sunk for-

ever into the mud of this dark and crowded street. "Sorry, Nell. 'Tis the trash heaps for us tonight."

Nell bit her lip. The trash heaps lay behind Tavern Row, in a narrow alley few cared to frequent. The last time they'd gone there, they'd had to fight off a pack of wild dogs.

"Tell you what," Rob said. "I'll walk up ahead and scout the place out." He led Nell to a dark hideaway near the end of the alley. "Wait here till you hear me whistle." He frowned at her. "And don't you go talking to no one."

She nodded, but Rob still felt uneasy. She was too trusting, was Nell. Too easy with strangers. But he'd done the best he could. She was safer in her hideaway than she would be with him.

He crept toward the first trash heap, which lay behind the Three Ravens, a tavern famous for its pork pies. Scavengers had already been at it, scattering dirt and refuse as they pawed through the pile. Rob could find nothing left worth eating. Even the bones were cracked and drained of their marrow. When he sniffed the air, however, he caught a greasy whiff of meat. The trimmings from the pork pies, perhaps? His mouth began to water.

He turned about in the darkness, searching for the source of the smell. At last he found a tall barrel standing against the side wall of the Three Ravens. He sniffed the air again. There was pork in that barrel, he was sure of it. The rich meat flavored the air, masking the dank smell of the river. Rob's belly squawked in delight.

Something to stand on, that's what he needed. He searched in the shadows till he found a split bucket lying in the dirt. He set it next to the barrel and used it to kick himself up.

Balanced precariously on the barrel's rough edge, he dipped his hand into the dark center. *Pork*, he thought. *Please let it be pork.*

He stretched his arm a little farther. His fingers struck something slimy. What was it? He plunged deeper into the barrel, then jerked his arm back. Pig guts! The barrel was full of them.

"Rob!"

Startled, he nearly tumbled headfirst into the barrel. He jerked back just in time and hit the ground hard.

"Oh!" Nell rushed up to him. "Are you hurt?"

Rob rubbed his shin and took a deep breath. "No bones broken, I guess." He glared up at her. "No thanks to you. I thought I told you to wait around the corner."

"I did, but then I heard somebody moaning. Somebody close."

Must've been a drunkard, Rob thought. *Good thing*

Nell'd had the sense to get away. He wiped his sticky arm on a frosty patch of dirt and staggered to his feet.

"I went to see who it was," Nell continued, "and—"

"You did what?!"

"—he needs our help, and so I—"

Rob gripped her thin shoulders. "Didn't you hear what I said, Nell? You're supposed to leave strangers alone!"

"But he's only a little boy."

Rob felt a sudden pang of sympathy. A little boy? He hesitated for a moment, then hardened his heart. He couldn't be expected to take care of every lost soul in London, could he? It was hard enough just taking care of Nell.

"His name's Kit," said Nell. "And he's hurt. He twisted his ankle, and—"

"I don't care what he done, or how old he is. You're to stay away from him, you hear?"

"But he needs us!"

Rob narrowed his eyes. "We've neither of us had more than half an apple to eat this day. We don't have time to worry about some lost boy."

"But—"

"Don't go sticking your neck out. That's what I say."

She twisted away from him. "Well, I think that's mean!"

"Nell—"

"He needs our help." She ran back down the alley.

Rob had half a mind to leave her to it and go on home. Serve her right if anything bad happened. She'd learn her lesson then.

Of course, if he didn't go after her, he'd likely worry all night long.

"Wished I never heard o' the girl," he muttered— and trotted after her.

He found Nell crouched in a dark corner at the edge of the alley, speaking softly to someone he couldn't quite see. "Your father will find you, just wait and see."

"But 'e don't know where I am!" The voice was soft, scared, uncertain.

"Mayhap I could find him for you," Nell said.

Rob stepped out of the shadows.

"Oh, Rob!" Nell's smile was so bright that he could see it even in this dim light. "I knew you'd help!" She turned back into the shadows. "Don't be frightened. 'Tis my friend, Rob. Tell him what you told me. He'll find a way to help you. I know he will."

Rob didn't know whether to be annoyed or pleased by her confidence in him.

A scrap of a boy peeked around Nell's cloak. "I'm K-k-kit," he quavered. "I come down to the docks to see me friend, but I 'urt me ankle, and then it got dark, and now I want to go back 'ome."

"We'll see you get there," Nell promised. "Won't we, Rob?"

Rob hesitated. He was tired and hungry, and the last thing he wanted was to walk about London with a boy on his back. But if he refused to help, he knew Nell and the boy would go on alone, and London was full of traps for babes like them. "If Kit here can tell us where he lives, I suppose there's no harm in taking him there."

He wasn't really breaking the rules, he told himself as he swung Kit on his back. Look after yourself and trust no one—that was his motto, true enough. But it wasn't as if this tiny boy could do anything to hurt him. And mayhap Kit's father'd be so grateful to have his boy back, he'd give them something to eat as a reward.

Soon Rob was so hungry, it was all he could do to keep moving. He shuffled down the streets, the boy clinging to his neck. Nell walked quietly alongside.

Thankfully, Kit had a good sense of direction. "This way," he'd say when they reached a corner. "That way." Finally, he pointed to a small hovel at the end of a long lane. "There. That's me 'ome."

Rob trudged down the lane. Kit didn't seem all that happy to be back on his own street. In fact, if anything, he seemed more nervous than ever.

Rob glanced uneasily at the dark, ramshackle houses that lined the lane. Perhaps Kit's nervousness was catching, for the back of Rob's neck soon began to prickle, and he felt as if eyes were watching him in every corner. When Nell lagged behind, he called her sharply back to his side.

"Don't stray, Nell. You don't want to go getting lost in this here place. Fair gives me the shivers, it does."

When they reached the tumbledown house that Kit called home, the boy slid to his feet and rapped on the warped wooden door.

"Who's there?" a heavy voice called.

"It's me," Kit sang out.

"Kit?" The door swung open, and Rob found himself looking at a heavy-handed butcher of a man. Was this little Kit's father?

"I brung two!" Kit cried. "Two!"

Rob didn't know what Kit was talking about, but he knew trouble when he heard it. He grabbed Nell's hand. "Come on, Nell!"

"Oh, no, you don't." The butcher man nabbed them, his hands quick as cats.

Rob kicked at the man. "Bite him, Nell! Scratch him!"

The butcher man shook them by their shoulders. "'Ere, 'ere! Enough of that—or I'll knock you to kingdom come!"

Nell went still, but Rob kept struggling. "What do

you want with us? We brought your boy back, didn't we?"

"You might say that." The man leered at him. "Or you might say 'e's the one as brought *you* back."

Kit puffed out his chest and grinned cheekily at Rob. "I fooled you! I fooled you!"

Rob glared at him but said nothing. His wits were better employed in figuring out how to escape.

"And as for why we want you," the butcher man said, "'tis no great mystery. There's many a man in Virginia as'll pay a pretty penny for a sprightly lad like you." He tightened his hold on Rob, then twisted his fingers into Nell's hair, making her gasp. "Why, there's even some poor souls as'll pay good money for her."

Virginia? It was worse than anything Rob had imagined. Panicked, he jerked himself free and hammered at the man's elbow.

With a bellow of rage, the man swatted at Rob's head. "I told you to keep still!"

An explosion of green went off in Rob's head.

Virginia, he thought dazedly. *Virginia.* And then everything went black.

Chapter 3

"Leave me alone." Rob groaned and turned his head toward the side of the ship, away from Nell.

Up and down, u-u-up and down. They'd been on the *Sparrow* for a week now, and the infernal rocking never stopped. Rob groaned again. Made him sick as a dog, the rocking did. Mayhap even sicker.

"Please, Rob," Nell pleaded, "if you'd just come up where the air is fresh, I'm sure you'd improve."

With what little strength remained to him after a week of seasickness, Rob glared at her. "I told you before, I don't want nothing to do with you."

"But Rob—"

He shifted around, putting his back to her. "Go away." It was her fault they'd been captured, her fault they were on their way to Virginia. Just now he couldn't stand the sight of her.

He closed his eyes, remembering the night they'd

been caught. Kit's father had brought them to the *Sparrow*, then haggled with the captain over their price. Still groggy from the blow he'd been dealt, Rob had heard enough to understand what was happening. The captain was planning to ship him and Nell across the Atlantic to Virginia, where he'd reap a handsome profit by selling them as servants to the highest bidder.

When the captain presented him with indenture papers, Rob had tried to fight his way free. Weak and dizzy, he was soon forced to sign his initials on the page. After Nell had made her mark, the second mate locked the two of them in the *Sparrow's* storeroom for the rest of the night. When they were finally freed, the ship had already set sail for Virginia.

Virginia. Just thinking about it made Rob's belly flop. He'd been too sick to listen overmuch to what the other passengers were saying about the colony, but he'd caught enough to confirm his worst suspicions. Virginia was a plaguey place where indentured servants labored all day in fields of tobacco. And that's what he and Nell were going to be: indentured servants, bound to serve their master without pay until they turned twenty-one.

Hah! thought Rob. *Twenty-one! Likely I'll be dead come Christmas. If I even makes it to Virginia in the first place.*

He opened his eyes and stared blankly into the dim twilight of the 'tween deck. One level down from the main deck, where the captain and his officers had their cabins, and one level up from the cargo hold, which held most of the supplies, the 'tween deck was crammed with sixty sweaty passengers, almost all of them men. Some of them looked—and sounded—as sick as Rob felt. Others, with more hardy stomachs, were playing cards and dice among the boxes and barrels. One man was even playing a pennywhistle, reminding Rob of Tavern Row.

What wouldn't he give to be back there!

'Tis all Nell's fault, Rob told himself again. *Didn't I say as no good would come of helping that scrawny little Kit? And I was right. Twisted ankle, my foot! That Kit was a regular rogue, and no mistake.*

Rob scowled at the side of the ship. The real mistake, he knew, had been his. Such a gudgeon he'd been, such a fool, to listen to a silly nine-year-old girl. He should have turned his back on her and her Kit. Better yet, he should have never taken her on in the first place, never promised to look after her. He'd been too softhearted, that was his problem. Too kind.

He buried his head between his knees, blocking out the groans of the other 'tween-deck passengers. Kindness was a virtue, his father had said. But since his father's death, Rob had learned the truth: Kindness was a luxury few could afford, a weakness that could cost you your life.

Well, he wouldn't make the mistake of being kind again. Deep in the belly of the *Sparrow,* Rob made a promise to himself—the same promise he made with every waking hour: *From now on I looks after meself. I'll not stick me neck out for no one.*

Nell prodded him with her elbow. "'Tis better up on deck, Rob. Truly it is."

He kept his head down.

"The air's fresh. Not like down here. And the sun's shining. . . ."

Rob sniffed to show his disdain, but the gesture backfired, for the smell of the 'tween deck—a pungent combination of sickness, sweat, and cold porridge—made his stomach quiver. He lurched to his feet.

"You're coming up?" Nell sounded pleased.

"Not cause o' you," Rob said, swallowing hard. "I just took it into my own mind to go up, see?"

Stomach heaving, he climbed the ladder to the open deck.

Nell was right, Rob decided. Up here the air was fresh and clear. The sun was so powerful bright, it made his eyes water. But it cheered him all the same. Even his stomach began to settle down.

Nell led him to the railing. When the ship rolled, he clutched at the rough, tarred web of rigging beside him. With the wind singing in his ears, he craned his neck and stared at the vast sails curving against the clear, blue sky.

"Have you ever seen anything so grand?" Nell asked.

"'Tis fair enough," Rob replied grudgingly. He might be feeling better, but that didn't mean all was forgiven. And the truth was that he was uneasy seeing nothing but sea and sky all around. Until he had come aboard the *Sparrow,* the widest stretch of water he had ever seen was the River Thames, which had seemed remarkable enough at the time. Yet the ocean that now stretched before him was greater than ten thousand such rivers. The sky, too, was enormous. No longer bounded by chimneys and rooftops, it circled down to the very edges of the sea.

Give me London any day, Rob thought. It might be full of rats and refuse and tricksters like Kit, but the city was home to him, and he could imagine no other. Yet here he was now, getting farther from London with every passing hour. The thought made his stomach lurch again.

When he looked at Nell, however, she was smiling. "We've no cause to be cheerful," he snapped. "Not when we're Virginia bound."

Nell tugged at her cape. "Mayhap Virginia isn't so bad as we've heard."

Rob snorted. "And mayhap I'm the king of Spain."

"But the other people on this ship weren't kidnapped," argued Nell. "I know some of them say they were tricked into signing an indenture. But many are here of their own free will."

"The more fool they," said Rob. "Anyone who goes to Virginia is putting his neck in a noose."

"Or his hand in a treasure chest," said a deep voice behind them.

Rob whirled around so fast, he almost made himself sick again.

It was a man who had spoken—a young man of perhaps twenty-one years, sitting cross-legged on the deck behind them. Even sitting, he was a considerable size, and the sharp green eyes under his plumed black hat said he knew how to use his strength.

In London, Rob would have been on his guard with such a man; indeed, he would have done his best to avoid him. But the rolling of the ship made it impossible to stride away in dignity. He could only clutch at the railing and scowl as Nell swept a curtsey to the stranger. "Good day, sir," she said.

The man's eyes filled with laughter, but his reply was polite enough. "Alan Larkin, at your service," he said, doffing his hat. "And who would you be?"

"Nell Cranston, sir. And this is my friend, Rob Brackett." Nell put her hands behind her back. "Please, sir, what is that in your hand?"

Larkin held up a spiky orange object the size of a small plum. "This?" He handed it to Nell. "Why, 'tis a piece of coral."

Nell ran a cautious finger along the blunt spikes. "Where did it come from?"

"The Caribee Islands."

"You've been there?"

"Not I. 'Twas a Spaniard who gave me this." He smiled at Nell. "It pleases you?"

"Oh, yes." Nell was clearly enchanted.

Rob, however, was anything but. In his experience strangers meant nothing but trouble—and friendly strangers, like this Larkin fellow, were trouble of the very worst sort.

Still, when Nell offered him the coral, Rob was too curious to turn it down. He rolled it between his fingers. For all its sunset softness, the coral was as hard as stone.

"'Twas alive once," Larkin told him, "growing under the sea. Or so they say." He took the coral from Rob and held it delicately between finger and thumb. "A marvel, is it not?"

"Is there coral in Virginia?" Nell asked.

"If there is, it's not yet been discovered." Larkin

pocketed the coral in his leather jerkin. "But there is much else to wonder at—furs and fish and fowl in great plenty. And dyes, of course, and pearls. And soon they will have wines and silks of their own manufacture. Or so they say."

Rob scowled at the stranger. "They say, too, that half the souls who go to Virginia are perished within the year."

Larkin grinned. "Your friend's a sour one," he said to Nell. "As it happens, though, he's behind the times. When the colony was run by the Virginia Company, there were many deaths, it is true. But Virginia is a royal colony now. Have you not heard?"

Rob shrugged. "'Tis all one to me."

"Virginia is a changed place under the king," Larkin persisted. "Though, to be sure, 'tis no place for cowards."

Rob bristled. "I'm no coward."

Larkin didn't seem to hear him. "As for me, I shall make my fortune there. You can be sure of that."

"Planting tobacco?" Nell asked, pulling her cloak around her.

He nodded. "'Tis the best commodity by far. They say a man can make a hundred pounds sterling from tobacco in just one year. And that's by his own labors alone. With servants, he may clear above five hundred pounds—a princely sum indeed. Of course," he added quickly, "I haven't any servants yet, only the land. But I shall buy them with the profits from my first crop, you can be sure of that. And at the end of five years"—his grin deepened—"I shall come back to England rich as the king himself."

Rob was unimpressed. "'Tis all very well for you, I suppose. You're not a servant. You haven't been kidnapped."

"Kidnapped?" Larkin arched an eyebrow in inquiry. When Nell explained what had happened to them, he shook his head. "'Tis a great pity you were taken in by those rogues. But who can tell? It may yet work to your advantage in the end."

Easy for him to say, Rob thought. *He isn't going to be slaving in someone else's tobacco fields.*

"There's many an opportunity in Virginia for those who have the skills," Larkin went on. "If you have a trade . . ."

"I can sew," Nell volunteered. "My aunt was a seamstress, and she taught me how."

"That's very good," Larkin told her. "Virginia has need of maids who are skilled in the domestic arts. And what of your companion?"

Rob glowered at him.

"Rob's father was a carpenter," Nell said. "And Rob worked under him."

"A carpenter, eh?" Larkin grinned. "Well, you're in

luck, then. Virginia's one vast forest, they say, so there's plenty of work for those who have skills with wood. Why, I hear carpenters earn three shillings a day."

Rob was intrigued in spite of himself. No carpenter in England was ever paid such high wages as that. "Three shillings a *day?*"

"In tobacco, of course. 'Tis the common currency in Virginia. Not that you'll be earning wages, of course. As servants, you'll be entitled only to bed and board. But you'll be practicing your trade, and that's what counts."

To practice his trade again—what a prospect! But why should he trust anything this man said? Rob thrust out his chin. "How do I know you're telling me the truth?"

"Ask any man here. They'll tell you the same," said Larkin. "The carpenters in Virginia are so desperate for apprentices, I daresay they'll be swimming out to meet you."

A cry came from the fo'c'sle, and two sailors trotted down the deck.

"They'll be hauling sail soon," Larkin said. "Best take another turn about the deck now, before the captain orders us back below."

"Below?" Rob echoed.

"Sailors don't like passengers frolicking about on

deck when there's work to be done," Larkin said. "If you take my advice, you'll stay out of their way."

For such a tall man, he was surprisingly agile. He swung to his feet, tipped his hat to them, and sauntered away.

Rob wasn't sure what to think as he watched Larkin go. Likely all he'd said was a pack of lies. But what if some of it were true? What if Virginia had work for carpenters? Rob thought with longing of what it would be like to hold a chisel in his hands again. To smell new-cut boards. To make something fine and lasting out of wood.

Beside him Nell twirled about the deck, busy with her own dreams. "Virginia sounds a grand place, does it not?" Without waiting for an answer, she went on, "I warrant we'll find a family who wants us there. You tell them you're a carpenter, and I'll tell them I can sew. . . . "

Her words brought Rob back to earth with a bang. He put out a hand and stopped her in mid-twirl. "Don't you be expecting so much, Nell. What Larkin says is too good to be true."

She looked at him uncertainly, teetering on one foot. "What do you mean?"

"I reckon we'll end up in the tobacco fields, Nell. And it's not likely we'll be together, either."

She stared at him, clearly upset. "You don't know that. Not for certain."

"'Tis what everyone says about Virginia."

"Not everyone," she argued. "Some say Virginia's like the Garden of Eden—"

"Virginia isn't going to be no earthly paradise," Rob scoffed. "The sooner you get over that notion, the better. Why, we'll be lucky if we last out the year."

Nell cried out in distress.

"No good going on about it," he said. "I'm just a-trying to prepare you, that's all. You're going to have to learn to look out for yourself, like I been telling you. 'Tis high time you stopped trusting every person you meet."

Nell clapped her hands over her ears.

Rob's frustration boiled over into anger. "All right, then—ignore me! Blowed if I care." He wheeled around and stomped away.

Chapter 4

Hot with temper, Rob started down the ladder to the 'tween deck. Nell wasn't being fair. It wasn't his fault they were headed for Virginia, was it?

He nabbed a place by one of the small 'tween-deck windows and stared at the blue-green waves, rolling endlessly to the far horizon. No, it wasn't his fault, but still, he shouldn't have gone and walked away from her like that. She was so small, and the ocean was so big. What if she lost her balance and fell in?

He glanced back at the ladder. Perhaps he should go up and make sure she was safe.

Then again, perhaps he shouldn't. *I'll not stick me neck out for no one.* That was the promise he'd made to himself. If he made an exception for Nell, they'd both live to regret it. She'd never learn to look out for herself if he kept doing it for her.

He did his best to settle down comfortably. Soon, however, the rolling sea took its toll on him. By the time Nell finally appeared at his side, he was slumped against the ribs of the ship, trying desperately to hold on to what little dinner he had left.

"Oh, Rob!" She knelt beside him. "I know you didn't mean to quarrel with me. 'Tis just that you're so sick. I see that now."

I meant every word, Rob wanted to say. But if he opened his mouth, he knew he'd be sick. Instead, he closed his eyes and, stomach flopping, tried to sleep.

After another week at sea, Rob began to feel better. Though he grumbled about the food the captain provided—"Pig slop, that's all it is. And that's what we are to him, I'll be bound: tiny pink pigs he's fattening up for market"—he admitted to himself the regular dollops of porridge and servings of salt fish were better fare than he'd managed to scrounge from Tavern Row. He hadn't eaten so well since before his father had died.

Nevertheless, he hated being on board the *Sparrow.* He hated the cramped 'tween deck, hated the limitless sea, hated the endless hours during which he had nothing to think of except what would happen once the *Sparrow* reached Virginia. When he said as much to Nell, she dismissed his fears. "I believe Master

Larkin," she said stoutly. "Virginia will be good to us. You wait and see."

Rob didn't bother replying. What was the point? She and Larkin would learn the truth soon enough.

Yet as the days passed, his frustration with Nell increased. He'd thought that once he stopped looking out for her, she'd learn to look out for herself. But already several weeks had gone by, and Nell didn't appear to have learned a thing. Against Rob's advice she made friends with the few women on the ship. Thieves, they were, being sent to Virginia as punishment, but when he said so to Nell on deck one day, she immediately rose to their defense.

"Molly Simpkins never stole those spoons. It was the steward who took them, but he wouldn't own up to it. And Alyce did steal a meat pie, but it was only to feed her little brothers because they hadn't had anything to eat for three days."

"That's not what I've heard," Rob said.

"Who says differently?"

Rob shrugged. "Other folks," he said, though all he'd heard was one sailor taunting the women for their crimes.

Nell turned rosy with exasperation. "'Other folks'? Rob, you never talk to anyone! If you did, you'd know the truth."

It was true enough that he talked to almost no one.

He avoided the few other boys his age on the ship, even the ones who were orphans like himself, and he had as little to do with the men as he could. Grizzled Sam Dobson, who was old enough to be his grandfather, could get no response from him, nor could Will Mayhew, whose shrill pennywhistle and lively storytelling had made him the most popular man on the ship.

"Why should I bother making friends?" Rob said to Nell now. "As far as I can tell, the first thing a friend does is rob you blind. I'm best off on me own—and so would you be, if you only had the sense to see it."

Ignoring her disappointed gaze, he walked away.

Rob hoped that Nell would eventually come around to his way of thinking, but as the weeks went by, she showed no sign of it. Time and again she gave a share of her porridge to the sick. She mended shirts for free. And she continued to believe every word Larkin said.

Rob couldn't get over it. *Thinks we'll be living in the Happy Isles, she does.*

What would become of her when they actually reached Virginia? What would become of them all?

Rob tried not to think about it.

The *Sparrow* reached Virginia on the first of May after eleven long weeks at sea.

"What did I tell you?" exclaimed Larkin as they sailed up the river toward Jamestown, the capital of the colony. "'Tis one vast forest!" He clapped Rob on the back. "A carpenter's paradise, eh?"

Rob was too awestruck to respond with anything more than a brief nod. He had not imagined there were so many trees in all the world. Of those close enough to identify, he saw oaks and some sort of pine, along with countless others whose names he did not know.

Nell came up beside him. Of late they had spent little time together, for she was busy with other friends, while he refused to make any. Sometimes he heard her making excuses for him to the others, saying that he was sick and low in spirits. Since bouts of seasickness hit him every time the ship encountered rough weather, he was in no position to argue with her, but it had annoyed him all the same. He hadn't asked her to defend him, had he? Why couldn't she just leave him alone?

Now, however, that was all behind him.

"What did I tell you?" Nell said softly. "Virginia *is* a grand place."

For once Rob didn't deny it. What he'd taken for a fairy tale had turned out to be true.

After the first few hours Larkin lost interest in the scenery and went down below for a nap. But Rob and Nell stayed by the railing all day, watching the land

slip by. In some places the trees marched right down to the riverbank. In others soft marshes fringed the river with tall reeds that harbored huge flocks of ducks and geese. Here and there the land had been cleared to make way for fields and rough farm buildings and small yards for chickens and cows. Twice they saw people in the fields and waved to them. In the end, however, these sparse signs of civilization served only to show how wild the place really was.

London-born and -bred, Rob found it unsettling to be so far from a city. Even the larger settlements he saw were no more than a few houses huddled together—a most unimpressive sight. But no doubt Jamestown would be bigger. James City, some of the men called it.

All the same, Rob was not eager to reach the place, for it was in Jamestown that he and Nell would be sold.

Guess I'll make out all right, he told himself. *With all these trees, it's clear enough they'll be wanting carpenters.*

But what would happen to Nell? If Larkin was right, she'd find a place as a seamstress. But Rob was still worried she'd end up in a tobacco field, the smallest servant of them all. *And everyone knows 'tis the littlest ones as get clobbered most,* he thought gloomily.

Still, why should he worry when Nell herself would

not? Cheerful as ever, she exclaimed over every new sight the river offered.

"Look!" she said now. She tugged at his sleeve and pointed down the river.

Rob struggled to follow her line of sight. "What is it?"

"A turtle. Can't you see?"

He squinted. "Where?"

"Climbing onto that log up there."

"I still can't—"

A cry from the rigging interrupted him. "Jamestown! Ja-a-a-mestown!"

Rob and Nell forgot the turtle. Holding fast to the railing, they craned their necks for a sign of the town and its fort. Behind them men crowded onto the deck, pushing and shoving in order to get the best view. Tempers ran high.

"Out of my way!"

"Quit shoving!"

"Your elbow's in my eye!"

When Jamestown came into sight, however, everyone fell silent.

"Why, 'tis no more than a village," someone said at last.

Stunned by the small size of the place, Rob shielded his eyes with his hand and surveyed the shore. A handful of people had gathered at the water's edge. Behind them stood a rickety wooden palisade containing a handful of half-timbered houses.

"Is that the fort?" one man wondered aloud.

"I hope not," said Larkin, sounding shaken.

But what else could it be? For there was nothing else on that shore save two rows of tiny thatched cottages and one small brick church. Aside from that Rob saw nothing but grass and sand and mud.

The sight chilled him to the bone. Despite all his forebodings, he'd never imagined a place as desolate as this. Pulling his gaze from the shore, he looked down at Nell. If Jamestown affected him this way, how must it appear to her?

"'Tisn't much of a place," she said doubtfully, "is it, Rob?"

"No," he said. "'Tisn't much of a place at all."

To his surprise, she smiled. "Look!" She pointed to the people on shore. "They're waving to us."

She leaned over the railing and waved back at them. Beside her Rob stood still and silent, staring at the bleak settlement that was to be their home.

Chapter 5

More than a week later, Rob, Nell, and the rest of the *Sparrow*'s passengers still had not set foot in Jamestown.

By law, they were told, all vessels arriving in Virginia had to wait at least ten days before disembarking passengers, in order that the authorities could certify they were free of contagion.

"We'll be on this stinking ship forever," Rob grumbled to Nell as they stood on the open deck, looking toward Jamestown.

After ten days with nothing to do but look at the town, they'd both grown rather used to the idea of settling in Virginia. Nell, who waved to every Virginian she saw, was convinced that she and Rob would find a family there who would take them both in. Rob wasn't at all sure she was right about that, but he was ready to take his chances on the place. Even the rotting palisade and the rickety houses no longer dismayed him. What better proof could there be that the Virginians were indeed desperate for carpenters? Rob could only hope they'd be desperate for seamstresses, too.

"Master Larkin says we'll be allowed to go ashore tomorrow," said Nell. "The captain told him so. And Will Mayhew says the same."

Sure enough, early the next morning two small boats came to ferry the *Sparrow*'s passengers to shore. Rob and Nell stood on the bright, windy deck for nearly an hour, waiting their turn.

"I wish I had a new dress," Nell said, looking down at her threadbare cape and gown, stained with saltwater, porridge, and tar.

"They'll have to take us as they find us," Rob told her. But he, too, wished he had new clothes, for every stitch on his back badly needed to be washed and patched.

At last they were sent over the side to the skiff that bobbed below. Waves splashed against the sides of the small boat, dowsing some of the passengers. Rob, who was squeezed into the bow, emerged on shore half soaked, his doublet dripping wet.

Two men with muskets bore down upon the skiff's passengers, directing them toward the palisade's open gate. "Freemen must assemble in front of the Governor's House. Bondservants along the side."

"Bondservants," Rob echoed. "That's us." He nodded at Nell. "Step smartly, girl. Might as well make a good impression."

After three months at sea, however, Rob found it difficult to follow his own advice. The ground rolled about like a bowl of custard, rising up to meet him, then plummeting down when he least expected it. Several times he stumbled, and twice he had to stop altogether. And he wasn't the only one having difficulties. All the *Sparrow*'s passengers were walking rather strangely.

"We've sea legs," said Larkin, who was attempting to balance a wooden chest on his shoulder. "'Twill pass in a day or so."

At last Rob and Nell reached the palisade gate. There a man with a sword at his side ordered them to stand with the other indentured servants alongside the Governor's House, which was a long, low building with a chimney at either end. As they waited for the last of the *Sparrow*'s passengers to join them, they watched the people milling about the palisade. Most were men in shabby clothes, but some had armor. A few women in worn dresses had gathered near a garden bed that stretched along the palisade's inner wall.

Nell pointed to the bed. "What grows there?"

"Tobacco," someone answered.

Rob glanced at the green shoots and at the women

standing nearby, but the buildings were what really held his interest. Close up, the palisade and its houses looked even less impressive than they had from the *Sparrow*. Only the Governor's House was in any way substantial. Rob, however, didn't think much of its construction. He reckoned it would be a tumbledown wreck in another ten years. Plenty of work for a carpenter there.

Rob was working out just what he'd do to fix the Governor's House when three men walked out of it. The first two carried muskets. The third one carried only a basket. Rob stared at him. Though he was dressed like the others in English clothes, he did not look English at all. He was slim and dark, with straight, black hair and broad, high cheekbones. Rob had never seen anyone like him before.

"An Indian." The word ran through the crowd of bondservants. "Look at the Indian!"

"Is he a servant?" someone asked.

"Must be," someone else answered. "He's wearing English breeches. Mayhap he's a Christian now."

A grizzled man next to Rob shook his head. "Once a savage, always a savage. That's what I say. Just look at that face!"

The three men were so close now that Rob could see the strange circles and lines that scarred the Indian's cheeks and chin.

"The Devil's mark," a man hissed.

Rob shivered.

"Aye, they're the Devil's own people," another man agreed. "I've heard they eat their own kind. . . ."

Before he could go on, a pompous man wearing a padded doublet and breeches called them all to order. His name, he said, was Master Dinwiddie, and they were all in his charge now. "Those of you who already belong to a particular master, come forward now."

All four women from the *Sparrow* stepped forward, along with several men.

"Follow me," Dinwiddie commanded. "The rest of you, stand quietly. Anyone who attempts to leave this area without permission will be whipped."

"Whipped? Just for stretching our legs?" a servant near Rob muttered. "What kind of country is this?"

"Silence!" Dinwiddie yelled.

Wary of upsetting the man further, Rob kept quiet and looked out across the compound while Dinwiddie took care of business at the far end of the Governor's House. The Indian and his companions had passed out of the palisade, but there was a sizable group of Virginians standing nearby, all of them men. A few were dressed more finely than the rest, in bright blue and green doublets that showed little sign of wear. But even the shabbiest Virginians studied Rob and his companions with watchful eyes.

They're the gentlemen as are going to buy us, Rob realized. It made his belly tighten, just looking at them. Which one would be his master?

"Look," Nell said. "Master Larkin is leaving."

Rob looked around. It was Larkin, sure enough. His chest balanced on his shoulder, he was passing through the palisade's other gate, the one that led to a small settlement on the bluff.

For the first time since they'd landed, Nell looked forlorn. "He didn't say goodbye."

"Likely they told him to keep away from us servants. I warrant he's too grand for us now." Rob spoke without emotion, not wanting to admit that he, too, was unsettled by Larkin's departure. Though he'd never been as easy with Larkin as Nell was, there was no denying he was a familiar face in this strange, new world. And now he was gone.

There was no time to fret, however, for Dinwiddie was now standing before them, beckoning the prospective buyers to his side. "We will, of course, proceed in an orderly fashion, with all due regard for rank. Master Pryor here will deal with the accounts, reckoning with Captain Deere as necessary." He pointed to the *Sparrow*'s captain and to a young man, scarcely bearded, who stood respectfully at his side.

The Virginians nodded. Apparently this procedure was familiar to them.

Dinwiddie singled out one of the best-dressed men and bowed fawningly before him. "Sir George, will you be so good as to choose your servants first?"

Sir George took his time, questioning several of the possible candidates and checking them over closely. Finally, he chose three servants—all brawny young men—and stepped over to settle his account with Master Pryor.

Dinwiddie now turned his attention to the next buyer. "Colonel Walsingham?"

And so it went, till the sun was high and hot in the sky and Rob's wet doublet dried and stiffened against his skin. During all that time he and Nell did their best to appear good-natured and hard-working, but none of the buyers showed any interest in them. What the Virginians wanted, it seemed, was grown men. The strong and healthy men first, and then the weaker ones—but always men.

"What if no one buys us?" Nell whispered, as yet another Virginian strode past them.

Rob glanced at the remaining servants, sickly-looking men who were well past their prime. "They'll want us soon enough, I warrant—as soon as they know that you sew and that I'm a carpenter."

One of the buyers, a stocky man with a brown beard and a calm face, stepped toward Rob. "A carpenter, you say? I've been looking—"

"Back away, Stanton!" Master Dinwiddie barreled toward them, showing none of the deference he'd displayed to the likes of Sir George and Colonel Walsingham. "Craftsmen have no call to be coming forward yet. There's many a greater man comes before you."

For a moment Stanton held his ground. Then, with a look of resignation, he gave way.

"Captain Holt," Dinwiddie called, "will you choose your servants?"

A bold man with a commanding air and a calculating eye, Captain Holt stepped forward. He was well armored, with a helmet over his long black hair and a solid breastplate over his jerkin. He was well armed, too, with a sword at his side and a heavy musket balanced on his shoulder. He strode down the line of servants, prodding arms and chests as he went.

Halfway down the line he turned to Master Dinwiddie. "We're down to the dregs, I see. Not a fit man among them."

"They are but tired by the journey—"

"I'm a soldier, Dinwiddie, not a fool. I've fought in Europe for half my life, and I know the stink of death when I smell it. These men will be in their graves before the month is out. I'd not pay a penny for the lot of them."

At the mention of graves, the line of servants shifted uneasily. Dinwiddie pointed to Rob. "What about this boy? He's healthy enough. And he says he's a carpenter."

Holt shrugged. "I need someone to tend my tobacco, not build me a house."

"But others need houses. You could keep him in the fields most of the year, then hire him out in the low season. You'd turn a greater profit that way."

Holt considered this, then jabbed a finger at Rob. "How old are you, boy?"

Rob was too startled to reply.

"Answer me!"

Rob found his voice. "Thirteen, sir. Nearly fourteen."

"Thirteen, eh?" Holt walked around him, eyeing him from every angle.

"The boy's a bargain, Captain." Dinwiddie was doing his best to make a sale. "Young people fare better in this climate than their elders do, you know. You're sure to get a full seven years and more from him. And of course—"

"Hold your chatter, Dinwiddie."

With that Captain Holt turned away. Relieved, Rob glanced at the small crowd of buyers who stood waiting. Among them was Stanton, the man who had spoken to Rob. He seemed pleasant enough—certainly more pleasant than Captain Holt. And he wanted Rob for his carpentry skills, so that was all right.

But what if Stanton didn't want to buy Nell, too? Rob looked down at her. She was standing so close to him that she was making it look as if they were a joint lot. What if she ruined his chances of finding a suitable master? Maybe he ought to put some more distance between them and make it clear that he was on his own.

As he took a step back from her, his conscience niggled at him. What would happen to her if they were separated?

That's her concern, he told himself firmly. After all, he'd told her from the beginning that they weren't likely to end up in the same family. Anyway, it was her fault they were in Virginia in the first place. He took another step back.

A heavy hand landed on his shoulder. "I'll take the boy," Holt said. "If the price is right."

Rob was horrified. So, to judge from her face, was Nell.

"I am certain we can reach an agreement," Dinwiddie said. "Shall we confer with Master Pryor?"

Nell latched onto Holt's arm. "Please, sir, we want to stay together. Won't you buy me, too?"

Holt shook her off. "Get away, girl! You're worthless to me." He stalked over to where the accountant and the sea captain were standing and began his negotiations.

Nell started after him. "But I—"

Rob dragged her back. "Leave him be, Nell," he whispered fiercely.

"But I want him to buy me!"

Rob was nearly as upset as she was, but he didn't let it show. "He won't do it, Nell. He said so, plain as can be. And judging from his face, he's not the sort who changes his mind."

"Then I'll follow you," she said desperately. "I'll wait till no one is looking, and then I'll run after you—"

"You'll do no such thing." Fear sharpened his voice. "Didn't you hear what they said? If you leave here without permission, you'll be whipped."

Holt strode toward them, a forbidding expression on his face. "We're leaving, boy." He started for the open gate. "Make sure you keep up."

When Rob went to follow him, Nell grabbed his arm. Before Rob could tell her to let go, a sudden blow separated them. Knocked off balance, Nell tumbled to the ground.

"That'll teach you to touch another's property, girl." Holt grabbed Rob's neck and jerked him upward. "As for you, boy, when I give you an order, I expect you to follow it. Do you understand?"

"Yes," Rob gasped.

"'Yes, *sir*.'" Up close, Holt's eyes were flat and colorless as the sea.

"Yes, sir," Rob repeated.

Holt released him. "Then march!"

Rob dared not disobey. Without another word he marched past the Governor's House, through the palisade gate, and away from Nell, who was still lying in the dirt.

Chapter 6

For what seemed like an eternity Rob trudged behind Holt, passing through settled lands into wilderness.

At last the man halted. "You're lagging behind," he growled.

Rob was too exhausted to defend himself. At the best of times he would have found it hard to match Holt's fierce pace, but with his sea legs buckling underneath him, he found it very rough going indeed. And his legs were not the worst of it. His head was still dazed by all that had happened since he had left the *Sparrow,* and he was worried sick about Nell.

He looked up to find Holt watching him. "You're not thinking of running off, are you, boy? For you'll not get far if you do. We've cleared the savages from these parts—but not the wildcats, nor the snakes, nor the bears. And the bears in Virginia are monstrous fierce. They've been known to eat a man alive."

Rob edged a little closer to Holt and his gun.

Holt shoved him forward. "From now on you'll walk in front, where I can keep an eye on you—and offer a little encouragement."

It soon became clear that Holt's idea of encouragement was to prod Rob sharply in the back every thirty yards or so. "That way, boy. Through those trees."

Rob plunged forward, too tired to care whether the trees in question were oak or birch or anything else. Carpenter or no, he'd had his fill of forest land on this journey.

Just as he felt he could go no farther, the forest gave way to an L-shaped clearing many acres wide, edged all around by trees. In the small arm of the L, a wooden paling straggled across a small bit of ground, enclosing three decrepit houses—if houses they could be called. To Rob's way of thinking they looked more like stables. It seemed they were inhabited, however, or at least one of them was, for a smudge of smoke hovered over its clay chimney. Beyond the paling, the fields stretched out into the distance, some half-covered with dead and dying trees, others empty of all but blackened stumps.

"Don't stand there gaping, boy." Holt prodded him again. "Inside the paling, and be quick about it. We've work to do before sundown."

The truth dawned on Rob. "You mean, you live here?"

"Yes." For once Holt slowed his pace. He gazed proudly across the barren clearing. "This is Hunter's Toyle. 'Twill bring me a fortune, this land."

In shocked silence Rob contemplated the black fields, the broken paling, the tumbledown houses, and the vast forest beyond them. To him it seemed the edge of the civilized world, the very last end of the earth.

"Come on, boy." Holt prodded him toward the paling.

They had covered only a few yards when a man came running out to meet them. "Cousin! You're back!"

Rob stared at the man trotting toward them. Holt's cousin, was it? Rob wouldn't have guessed they were kin. To be sure, they both had dark hair and light eyes and uncommonly long noses. Holt, however, was as massive as an English oak, while his cousin was delicate in frame and face, with a chin that trembled like an aspen.

Holt stopped short. "What were you doing in the house, Fanshawe?"

"I—I was just checking to see how our dinner was coming on. 'Tis nearly ready—and just in time, too. Not that I would have started without you, of course." Fanshawe smiled ingratiatingly at his cousin.

Holt did not smile back. "The field by the creek—you've hilled it?"

"Nearly."

Holt said softly. "What do you mean, nearly?"

"I've hilled nearly half of it."

"Half?"

"Well, perhaps only a quarter," Fanshawe said nervously.

"A quarter, is it?" Holt was bellowing now. "God's blood, man, but you try my patience!"

Fanshawe paled. "I—I could not work. My head ached so."

Rob could sympathize. His head, too, was aching, and he was dizzy with hunger. Still, he knew better than to call attention to himself. Holt would surely take it amiss if he did.

His body, however, betrayed him. As the smoke from the chimney drifted their way, his belly let out a long and wild growl. The two men turned toward him.

"Who is this?" Fanshawe asked.

"Our new servant."

Fanshawe frowned. "But he's only a boy."

Holt started toward the dwelling with the smoking chimney, dragging Rob along behind him.

Fanshawe trailed after them. "I thought we agreed on a man, Holt. A full-grown man to ease the work."

There was a note of panic in his voice. "What good is a boy to us?"

"He was the best of the lot," Holt said. "And I'll have no complaints from you, you lazy beggar. If you worked harder, we wouldn't be needing another servant."

"Gentlemen aren't supposed to work like field hands," Fanshawe retorted. "Grubbing about in the dirt, fetching their own water, living like pigs in a sty—what kind of life is that?"

Holt turned on him, his face savage with anger. "'Tis my life, cousin. For years I've been mired in blood and muck, a soldier for hire. To rise to captain, I risked life and limb abroad while you stayed home and played the pretty part of a gentleman. And all because you were the first son of a first son, and I was the fifth child's brat." He spat on the ground at Fanshawe's feet. "Well, you and I are on the same level now. You'd best get used to it."

Fanshawe shook his head stubbornly. "You didn't tell me it was going to be like this, Holt. I'd never have left England if I'd known."

"You'd have stayed in the one moldering manor you hadn't gambled away, I suppose. A fine estate that was, to be sure. Miss Rawlings of Cotting Hill would have been proud to be mistress there, don't you think?"

"You leave Miss Rawlings out of it!" Fanshawe shouted, his cheeks on fire.

Holt shrugged. "As you wish. I'll merely remind you that a certain young lady will be most impressed if you manage to make your fortune in Virginia." He leaned toward Fanshawe, speaking slowly for emphasis. "And she need never know you made it with your own lily-white hands."

Fanshawe stared back at him as if into the eyes of a snake. After a moment he said uncertainly, "You're quite certain we will turn a profit?"

"A profit? A fortune, rather!" Holt collared Rob and started again toward the dwelling.

Fanshawe followed after them. When he spoke again, it was with considerably less defiance. "I suppose even a boy is worth something. At the very least he can help us keep an eye on the girl."

Rob's ears pricked up. A girl?

"Such an infernal nuisance she is, always looking to run away," Fanshawe continued.

Rob glanced about him. Run away to where? He could see nothing but forest.

"She'll not run while Hades is here," said Holt, reaching the house. "An English mastiff is match for anyone, eh, Hades?"

An enormous dog rose from the doorstep. Rob stopped in his tracks. Infamous for their merciless bite, mastiffs had been known to take on bears—and win. Because of their cruel nature, most were kept chained. Hades was no exception, Rob was glad to see.

"Easy now, Hades," Fanshawe said. The dog backed away from the door but remained standing.

"Down!" Holt commanded.

Hades flattened himself in the dirt. Holt stepped over him, dragging Rob in his wake. "Into the house, boy."

Rob stumbled over the threshold and then, disoriented, came to a halt. His eyes, used to the bright sunlight outside, could not see a thing in the windowless house.

"Girl!" Holt bellowed.

"I expect she'll be up in the loft," said Fanshawe.

"She'd better be."

Rob heard feet scampering above him. That must be the girl, then, coming down from the loft. He strained to see her in the darkness. Was she an orphan like him? Was she a Londoner?

Perhaps they could join forces. Perhaps together they could outwit Hades. . . .

His vision began to clear. The girl was standing in front of the hearth. She was about his height. But she was darker, he thought, unless that was a trick of the light.

He blinked several times. Now he could make out

the girl's features: the high cheekbones; the straight black hair. He'd been right—she was dark, as dark as stained oak, or chestnuts in autumn. In fact . . .

Rob drew back in alarm.

The girl was an Indian.

Chapter 7

Holt thrust his trencher toward the Indian. "Another helping, girl."

"And for me as well," said Fanshawe.

Wordlessly the girl filled both trenchers with rabbit stew and set them back on the table. She then returned to her place on the dirt floor, a few feet away from Rob.

Unlike Holt and Fanshawe, Rob could do no more than pick at his dinner. Although he was hungry, he was too terrified to eat.

An Indian. He was sitting beside an Indian. Fear parched his throat, making it hard to swallow. *The Devil's own people*. That's what the man in Jamestown had called the savages. And Rob was more than willing to believe him.

To be sure, he had not expected the Devil's kin to

be so demure. The girl beside him kept her head low. She met no one's eyes. And she could not speak. Not in English, not in her own language. As they'd sat down to their meal, Holt had told him that she was mute—and rather slow in the head, as well.

Rob glanced sideways at her. She was about his own size and weight, he guessed, though it was hard to tell because she was dressed in clothes that were much too large for her: a man's shirt, a ragged skirt, and a stained apron tied tightly around her waist. Her dark braids were tied with strips of faded fabric. To his surprise her round cheeks were faintly pitted, just as his own were. In that way, at least, they were alike: They both had survived the smallpox.

Even so, Rob decided it would be foolish to let his guard down. Everyone knew that savages were a treacherous lot. What if the girl took it into her head to kill them all?

Rob edged a few inches farther away from her. He longed to be sitting next to Fanshawe, or even Holt, both of whom had swords to defend themselves. They'd made it quite clear, however, that his place was on the floor.

He stared at his stew, now growing cold and glutinous. He must eat it somehow, for who knew when he'd get his next meal? Keeping a close watch on the girl, he took one spoonful and then another. Bite by bite he forced the stew down. As he scraped the bottom of his trencher, Holt rose from the table. "'Tis high time we were back in the fields."

Fanshawe's spoon clattered against his trencher. "Already?"

Holt banged his fist on the table. "You will work when I tell you to work. All of you!"

He rose from his chair and donned his armored breastplate. As Fanshawe slowly followed suit, Holt grabbed hoes from a pile by the door and handed them out—long ones for himself and his cousin, shorter ones for Rob and the girl. He then led them out the door, past Hades, the mastiff, who bared his teeth and lunged at the Indian girl. Eyes wide, she leaped back, nearly tripping on her overlong skirt.

"Down, Hades!"

At Holt's command the dog dropped to the ground. Holt grabbed the girl and shoved her forward. The dog tensed but did not spring. "He knows who his master is," Holt said with satisfaction.

Rob glanced at the girl, who was rigid with fear. Small wonder, with a beast like that baying for her blood.

"That's right, boy," Holt said to Rob. "Get a good look at her, here in the sunlight. You'll be keeping watch over her, as we do. And you'd better watch her closely, boy, because if you let her escape, I'll flog you." Holt's cold, flat eyes fixed on Rob. "A soldier's flogging, boy. You'd be lucky to survive it. Do you understand me?"

Whatever stirrings of sympathy Rob felt for the Indian dissolved into fear for his own skin. "Yes, sir."

"Good," said Holt. He led them through the gate.

By the time they reached the stumpy fields, Rob's lungs were working like bellows, for he was unused to the heat of a Virginia afternoon. It hadn't been so bad when he'd been following Holt through the forest, but here in the open it was like a baker's oven—and they hadn't even started hoeing yet.

Holt did not stop till they reached the farthest edge of the field. "You know how to hill, boy?"

"No, sir."

"He's just off the ship," Fanshawe pointed out.

Holt gave his cousin a withering glance. "Since you're so wise, cousin, I'll leave you to explain it to him." With that, he stalked off to another corner of the field.

"Go on, girl," Fanshawe said to the Indian. "Follow him."

When she looked at him blankly, he pointed toward Holt and loudly repeated the order. "Follow him."

After a moment the girl moved off. Fanshawe turned toward Rob. "Now, then, boy—"

Rob was tired of being called "boy." "Me name is Rob, sir."

"Is it now?" Fanshawe jammed his hoe into the earth. "There was a Rob in the first lot of servants, too."

The first lot? What did he mean?

"A big man he was, and brawny. Well worth the price. Or so it seemed at the time."

Rob wet his lips. "What happened to him, sir?"

"He died. Like all the rest of our servants." Fanshawe shook his head. "We came with six last winter, and they all died. Cursed bad luck we've had, eh, boy?"

Rob nodded, for Fanshawe clearly expected him to agree. Privately, however, he was shocked. Six servants dead in one year! What had Holt and Fanshawe done to them? Worked them into their graves?

"'Twas the fever that did it," Fanshawe continued. "Though I daresay the flogging Holt gave to the woman didn't help. Nearly killed her, he did, and then the fever finished her off."

Despite the heat of the sun, Rob shuddered.

"Get on with it, Fanshawe!" Holt shouted from across the field.

Fanshawe sighed heavily. "Listen closely, boy," he told Rob. With his hoe he pointed back to the distant paling. "We've started the tobacco in a bed near the house, to protect it from frost. In a week or two, when the plants are big enough, we'll set them out in the fields. First, though, we have to make hills for them. Like this." He cut sharply into the ground with his hoe and spread the loosened earth over his foot. "Take care not to pack the soil too tightly."

He kept heaping earth over his foot until the pile reached his knee. "Now I take my foot out—see? Then I pat the top of the hill with my hoe. And then I move on. Do you follow?"

"Yes, sir."

"Let's see you do it."

Under Fanshawe's close supervision, Rob made one hill, and then another, and then yet another, till he was so drenched in sweat, he couldn't see straight.

"All right, boy," said Fanshawe. "Keep making those hills every yard or so till sundown."

Rob didn't think he could last for another hour, let alone till the sun set. But Holt was watching him closely, so he didn't dare rest.

For a while he kept a tally of the hills he made. After he reached twenty, however, each hill blended into the next, and he no longer had a marker to judge his progress. Time, it seemed, had stopped; even the blazing sun stood still.

At long last, however, the shadows began to lengthen, and the day began to cool. When it was so dark that Rob could no longer see the other end of the field, Holt ordered him to stop. They all trooped over to the creek, where they washed their hands and faces before returning to the house. There they made a small supper of cold rabbit stew.

A mangy sort o' meal this is, Rob thought as he forced it down. Nowhere near enough food to fill a body after working in the fields all day.

If the meal did little to lessen his exhaustion, it did much to revive the men. From the shelf by the hearth they took down clay pipes and lit them from the faint embers of the fire. As they talked of the money they hoped to make, heavy blue smoke drifted up from their pipes and filled the room, tickling the back of Rob's throat.

After a while Fanshawe went to the door and looked out. "So the Freeds are still in Jamestown, and Morgan's away in Archer's Hope. That leaves just the four of us here in Hunter's Toyle." He fiddled with his pipe, then glanced out the door again. "I hope we are not attacked."

"By whom? The savages?" Holt snorted. "Their villages lie in ashes, cousin. There's not an Indian within five miles who would dare to attack us. And what else can threaten us here within the paling?"

This seemed to reassure Fanshawe. At any rate, he came back to the table and sat down by his cousin.

Rob tried to listen to their conversation, but he

could barely keep himself awake. He glanced about the cramped dwelling, searching for a place to bed down for the night. The large bedstead in the corner was obviously meant for Holt and Fanshawe, and the Indian girl had already vanished up into the loft.

Guess it's the floor for me. Rob settled himself down near the door and closed his eyes.

The next thing he knew, a boot was prodding his backside. "Get off the floor, boy."

"A body has to sleep somewheres," Rob protested drowsily.

Holt hauled him upright. "You'll make your bed in the loft."

Wide-awake now, Rob stared at him. "But that's where the Indian sleeps!"

"That's where the *servants* sleep," Holt corrected him.

"But she's a savage," Rob said. "And I'm English. You can't put us both—"

"Get up there, boy. Now!" Holt slapped a wooden pail into Rob's hand. "And take your chamber pot with you."

Rob discovered he was even more afraid of Holt than he was of the Indian. Heart pumping, he climbed up the pole ladder. Setting down the pail, he laid himself down in the loft, taking good care to keep as far away from the girl as possible.

He heard boots clatter to the floor below him. Sheets flapped; a mattress rustled. Holt and Fanshawe were settling in for the night. Soon the small house shook with their snoring.

Up in the loft Rob lay awake. His body was tired, tired beyond imagining, but this time as he settled in for sleep his mind would not let him rest. What would happen to him here in Hunter's Toyle? Where was Nell? Would he ever see her again? Would she end up like the servants who had slept in this very loft—dead and gone within the year? The questions went on and on. And all the while the Indian girl lay only a few feet away from him. Was she planning an attack?

In time, however, his weary body won out over his fearful mind, and he fell asleep.

Later that night Rob awoke to the choked sound of near-silent crying. Hardly more than breathing, it was, and still it broke his sleep.

Nell, his tired mind said. For that was how Nell had been crying when he'd found her huddled in that dark London alley.

But then he remembered that he wasn't in London. He was in Virginia, in Hunter's Toyle. So who was crying?

Rob lay still in the darkness and listened. The

girl—that's who was crying. The Indian. And even now that he was awake, she still sounded like Nell—Nell alone and abandoned and frightened beyond words.

What should he do?

Even as the question formed in his mind, Rob rejected it. *I've enough on me plate without worrying about anyone else. Especially an Indian.*

But it wasn't till the crying stopped that he finally fell back asleep. And when he slept, he dreamed that he was back in London—and that Nell was crying in the gutter because he wouldn't take her in.

Chapter 8

For five long days they hilled the fields, till at last the work was done.

When Rob awoke on the sixth day, he wondered what they would do next. They couldn't move the tobacco shoots into the hills, for that, he'd been told, required rain—and plentiful rain, at that. Otherwise, the tender plants would not take root, but would wither and die under the fierce Virginia sun.

"Get down here, boy!" Holt's voice shook the frail dwelling. "Else you'll not break your fast this morn— or the next."

Rob rolled to his feet. The hilling might be finished, but Holt would have no trouble finding other work for him to do, and doubtless it would be as mindless and taxing as hilling had been. Hoeing Indian corn, perhaps. Or weeding the tobacco bed.

Wearily, Rob descended the ladder. From now on, it seemed, his life would be one long stretch of hard labor. Indeed, he had almost forgotten that there was any world but this one, where Holt was master and he was drudge.

Downstairs he found Holt and Fanshawe sitting at the table, eating porridge. The Indian girl silently handed Rob a trencher of his own.

He took it from her and retreated some distance away. After he'd heard her crying that first night—crying like Nell—he'd lost his fear of her. But she still made him uncomfortable.

She's more like a ghost than a girl, he thought. *She never looks no one in the eye, never even says so much as one word.* Yet for all that she put him in mind of Nell, which troubled him.

Holt rose from the table. "Put that trencher down, boy, and let's be off."

Rob stared at Holt. The man was dressed much more finely than usual, in dark blue breeches and a clean linen shirt, and his armor looked freshly polished.

"Where are we going, sir?" he asked.

Holt ignored him. Musket in hand, he stalked out the door.

Fanshawe picked up his own gun, lighter and leaner than Holt's. "We are going to divine service in Jamestown, boy. 'Tis the Sabbath, you know."

Rob hadn't known. Here the days were all alike; it was hard to keep track of them. But even if he had known it was Sunday, he would not have expected to be going to services. Holt did not seem the sort of man who would spend time in church when there was money to be made elsewhere.

"There are two services, one in the morning and one in the afternoon," Fanshawe went on. "If we miss either one, we will be fined three shillings a head."

So that was it. Holt hadn't turned pious. He just hated losing money.

Before Rob could take another spoonful of porridge, Fanshawe snatched his trencher away from him. "Didn't you hear what I said, boy? There's no time to lose."

"My clothes aren't fitting for church," Rob protested.

"Your garb is good enough for the servants' row," Fanshawe told him. "Now come, make haste. Holt will be waiting for us, and the Freeds as well."

The Freeds, father and son, lived in the dwelling next to their own. They owned the only boat in Hunter's Toyle. Though Rob had not yet spoken with them, he'd seen them toiling in the fields on the far side of the paling. From Fanshawe, Rob had gathered there had once been another son to help with the work, but he had died.

"What o' Captain Morgan, sir?" Rob asked. Morgan was their only neighbor aside from the Freeds. Wearing a bedraggled black hat with a jaunty air, he liked to visit with Fanshawe. Holt, however, didn't think much of the friendship. Morgan spent more time gaming and drinking than he did planting, Holt said, and ever since his servants had died it had been clear that he'd never amount to anything

"He is . . . er . . . indisposed," said Fanshawe. "And that's enough questions from you, boy!" He hustled Rob and the girl past Hades and out the settlement gate.

They found Holt down by the creek, helping the Freeds launch their small, flat-bottomed boat. As they all crammed aboard, Holt handed Rob a bucket. "Start bailing, boy. And keep an eye on the girl. I'll not have her jumping out and running away."

Rob nodded, but as the boat glided down the creek, he was thinking more about Nell than about the girl beside him. Fanshawe had said that everyone within reach of Jamestown had to attend divine service, so Nell was likely heading there now, too. For the first time since Holt had brought him to Hunter's Toyle, Rob had something to look forward to.

They reached Jamestown just in time for the service. As they scurried past a row of cottages, Rob couldn't help thinking how much more impressive the town seemed to him now that he'd spent nearly a week in the wilderness. Two muddy streets ran east to west, both of them lined with wooden houses that looked considerably more comfortable than the huts at Hunter's Toyle. At least a hundred people must be settled here. Was one of them Nell?

When they entered the church, Rob and the Indian girl were directed to the back, where the colony's servants stood in rows against the wall. Rob hardly had time to take his place among them before the service began.

Although the minister had a deep, sonorous voice, Rob paid little attention to it. It was not that he did not believe in God; like everyone else he knew, he accepted the existence of the Almighty. But he'd come to the conclusion that the Almighty was not overmuch interested in him. Though he'd prayed for help when his father had died, his prayers had not been answered. He hadn't bothered praying since.

Now he let the minister's words roll over him as he scanned the rows of servants, searching for Nell.

Most of the servants were male, he discovered, perhaps as many as nine in ten. Almost all of them looked English, but here and there Rob saw a few Indians, including the man he'd seen coming out of the Governor's House six days ago. He also saw a few men and women with skin as black as ink. There were a few folks like them in London, too, he remembered. Moors, they were, from Africa. He'd heard Holt say they could stand the sun better than Englishmen could, but Rob thought they looked as tired as he was.

He did not see Nell.

Wondering if she'd had better luck than he had, he turned his attention to the benches where the grander folks sat. Dressed more brightly than the servants, with lace collars and fine sashes and feathered hats, they, too, ran mostly to men. At length, however, he spied a young girl who, from the back at least, looked like Nell. He stared at her head, willing her to turn and look back at him. She did not move. He had to wait till the service was over and the parishioners filed past him before he knew the truth: She wasn't Nell.

Rob followed the other servants outside, where the sun was hot and hazy. Despite the heat, few parishioners showed any inclination to hurry off between services. Seeking a cooler place to stand, Rob wandered over to the shady side of the churchyard, where Holt and Fanshawe were swapping news and stories with the other men.

Rob turned to go before they saw him. Then he had another thought. *Mayhap Larkin is in this crowd—and mayhap he knows where Nell is.* Rob edged closer.

"There's a storm coming today, or I miss my guess," he heard one gentleman say.

"Can't come soon enough to suit me," another replied. "My tobacco's near ready to plant."

"I say, is it true Dickenson's given up?" asked a man in a green feathered hat.

"Aye, 'tis true," a ferret-faced man said. "He'd lost too many servants and was having too much trouble with the others. Not a lick of work would they do. Two of them were whipped by the court for foul language last winter, do you remember? And just last month a third was branded for thieving."

"The more brandings, the better," Holt said. "It keeps the servants from getting cocky."

The men around him nodded. "A dozen years back we used to hang them if they stole so much as a pair of shoes," one said. "Now, that's what I call discipline."

It seemed Holt wasn't the only Virginian who was hard on his servants. In the shade nearby Rob shivered.

"Didn't Dickenson have a runaway, too?" asked the man in the green hat.

"That he did," said the ferret-faced man. "Not that he ran very far. They found him in the woods a month later, dead in a ditch."

"Serves him right," Holt said.

Unable to stomach any more, Rob began to back away. By now he had seen enough to know that wherever Larkin was, it wasn't here. He was better off searching for news of Nell on the servants' side of the churchyard.

As he passed the church steps, he saw two men from the *Sparrow* talking. Perhaps they would know something about Nell. It seemed worth asking, anyway, though he could not remember their names.

To his chagrin, they did not recognize him. "Away with you, boy," one said. "Do not disturb us with your prattle."

Too proud to argue with them, Rob walked away. Surely he would find other people from the *Sparrow* here who would hear him out. But as he surveyed the crowded churchyard, his doubts began to grow. There weren't that many people he recognized, and none of them were people who were sure to recognize him in return. For the first time Rob wished that he had been a bit friendlier to his fellow passengers on the *Sparrow*.

Never mind, he told himself. *It would've all come to the same in the end. Catch them lifting a finger to help, whether they knows me or not!*

"Why, 'tis the sulky lad from the ship," a voice beside him said.

Rob looked up and found Will Mayhew, the *Spar-*

row's pennywhistle player, standing beside him. A short, fair man with a shock of hair like thatched straw, he had a grin as wide as a milk pail.

"Cat still got your tongue, then?" he asked Rob cheerfully.

Annoyed by the teasing, Rob nearly turned his back on Will but remembered just in time that he couldn't afford to spurn anyone from the *Sparrow* just now. As politely as he could, he explained that he was searching for Nell.

"The lass as was aboard the ship?" Will's eyes were kinder than Rob would have expected. "Sorry, lad. Don't believe I've seen her. But mayhap they have." He led Rob over to another couple of men from the *Sparrow,* who were talking in hushed whispers about the way their masters treated them.

"They think we're beasts, they do," the younger one was saying. "No better than bloody oxen! They can whip us half to death, and no one will speak a word against them."

Neither of them had seen Nell.

"You might look about for someone her own age, like," the older one suggested. "Mayhap they'll know more."

"'Tis a sound notion," Will agreed.

Rob thanked them—they hadn't been much help, but they'd shown more concern than he'd expected—

and excused himself from their company. If he was going to ask boys his own age for help, he'd best do it on his own.

Although there had been a fair number of boys attending the service, none of them were gathered nearby. Rounding the corner, he found them behind the church, a pack of a dozen boys standing in a tight circle.

"They're not really people, you know," Rob heard one boy say. "They're more like animals."

"Like dogs!" another voice cried.

The pack of boys burst into raucous laughter.

"Bark, dog! Bark!" a boy cried.

The crowd took up the chant. "Bark, dog! Bark!"

When some of the boys doubled over with laughter, Rob was able to see the object of all this taunting. At the center of the circle stood the Indian girl, head bowed so low, her chin nearly touched her chest.

"Bark, dog! Bark!"

The boys began to yank the girl's hair, pulling the braids loose and jerking her head back. She opened her mouth, as if crying aloud, but made no sound.

"Bark, dog! Bark!"

Rob felt sick to his stomach. He had no love for the girl, but she had done nothing to deserve such treatment. It put him in mind of a day he had almost forgotten, a winter's day when he was ten years old and a bunch of boys had cornered an old beggarwoman outside his father's shop. Howling with laughter, they'd pelted her with mud and stones. While Rob had watched tensely from his bench, his father, a stout cudgel in his hand, had strode out into the street. The boys had scattered at the sight of him. "Cowards, they be," his father had said. "Any who prey on the weak are cowards at heart. Mind you remember that, Rob."

What would his father say now?

Likely he'd go to the girl's rescue, Rob thought. *But that don't mean that I'm bound to do the same.*

His father, after all, had been a grown man and his own master, while Rob was only a boy and a servant. If he tried to stop the boys from going after the Indian girl, he'd likely find himself their quarry instead.

I've got to look after meself, Rob decided. Yet as he listened to the boys snickering and chanting and barking, somewhere deep inside he felt ashamed.

"Boy!" Holt collared him. "Where is the Indian? If you've let her run off, I'll flog you."

"Sh-she's over there, sir," Rob stammered.

Holt released him and stalked toward the pack of boys who had surrounded his servant. "I'll break your necks if you've damaged my property!" he roared.

At the sound of his voice the boys ran, leaving the girl alone on her knees.

"Get up," Holt commanded her. When she didn't move, he roughly jerked her to her feet.

Rob felt sick all over again, especially when he saw the tears running down the girl's face. But there was nothing he could have done, he reminded himself. Not without risking himself, anyway.

Within moments Holt had him by the collar again. "Didn't I tell you to watch over her, boy?"

"Yes, sir," Rob gasped.

Holt twisted Rob's collar tight and marched them both to the shady side of the church. "From now on you'll stay right here, where I can keep an eye on you." He backed them both against the church wall and went back to his companions.

Chapter 9

That Sunday afternoon Jamestown was like a kettle coming to a boil. Inside the church brows glistened, hair curled, stiff lace fell limp. When the second service finally came to an end, the parishioners gratefully unstuck themselves from their benches and poured out the doors, hoping for relief. Yet even under the trees the air was hot and heavy and still.

Holt pulled Rob and the Indian girl away from the crowd soon after they appeared at the door. "I'll not have you gabbling away the afternoon. 'Tis time we went back to Hunter's Toyle."

"What of the Freeds?" Fanshawe asked. "Are we not returning in their boat?"

"No. The son is fainting sick, and the father will not leave him." It was clear Holt disdained such devotion. "We will walk back without them."

He marched them through Jamestown at a smart pace, making no allowances for the heat. "I'll have no laggards in my company," he warned them. "Keep up, or it will be the worse for you."

Soon they entered the forest. Rob's head thrummed as he pondered the news he'd heard on his way out of church from old Sam Dobson of the *Sparrow*. Gaunt-cheeked and dull-eyed, he'd told Rob that some of the *Sparrow*'s passengers had been sold downriver.

"Do you know if Nell Cranston was among them?" To prod the old man's memory, Rob added, "She was the only girl on the ship. Nine years old, and—"

Dobson held up a leathery hand. "I remember, lad. But I've told you all I know."

"Mayhap I could ask Master Pryor." *If Holt lets me have a moment to meself.*

"Master Pryor?" Dobson grimaced. "He'd not tell you a thing. And no good would come of your asking. Might as well face the truth now, lad: One way or t'other, you'll not see the girl again. Why, there's one from the *Sparrow* as is dead already."

"Who?" Rob asked.

"Master Larkin. Bit by a snake, he was, this Friday past."

Larkin, dead? Rob shook his head in disbelief.

"Oh, 'tis true, lad. Virginia's a cruel, hard place. Wished I'd a known that sooner, afore I signed to come here." The man sighed. "Best put the girl out of your mind, lad, that's what I say—and Master Larkin, too."

Good advice, perhaps, but Rob had trouble taking it. Even now, as he struggled to keep up with Holt, the shock of Larkin's death stayed with him. It was only six days since they'd all left the *Sparrow,* and now Larkin—clever, confident Larkin—was in his grave.

His grief for Larkin made him more worried than ever about Nell. Was the man from the *Sparrow* right? Had she been sold downriver? Was she even still alive?

"Keep up," Holt cried, "all of you, or I'll leave you to the bears and the wolves!"

Rob shuddered and pressed on.

At last they reached a large, flat rock that Rob vaguely remembered from his first trip to Hunter's Toyle. Here Holt stopped and turned around. Seeing only Rob and the Indian, he roared after his cousin, "Fanshawe! Where are you?"

A distant voice responded, but it was so far away, they could not make out the words.

They waited by the rock till Fanshawe trotted up to them, balancing his gun against one shoulder. Sweat ran in small rivers down his body. "Blasted heat!" he gasped, collapsing at the foot of a tree.

Holt shrugged. "I've known worse. As a soldier in the Lowlands I often marched all day—"

"I am not a soldier, Holt." Puffing hard, Fanshawe

fingered the limp lace at his cuffs. "I am a gentleman. And I tell you, I hate this filthy place!"

"This 'filthy place' will make you rich," Holt said.

"So you say." Fanshawe's breath came more easily now, but his face was still crimson. "All it's done so far is beggar me. 'Tis enough to make a man give up and go home."

Holt glowered at him. "We'll not go home till our pockets are full."

"We'll die from the heat first," Fanshawe muttered.

Holt ignored him. "Think of it, Fanshawe! Money enough to restore your family's estates—and your family's honor."

"Only if it rains," said Fanshawe.

Holt's eyes burned as bright as the sun. "I tell you, it will rain." He pointed upward with his musket. "Look at that sky!"

Fanshawe glanced upward. So did Rob. Dark clouds were scudding over the tops of the trees.

"Rain." On Holt's lips, the word sounded like gold. "That's what those clouds mean." He settled the musket against his shoulder. "We'll make our fortune yet, cousin! Now march, all of you, and be quick about it!"

In England the rain fell gently; in Virginia it hammered at a body like fine nails driving into wood.

And that's what I feels like, Rob thought. *A piece o' wood what's been warped and battered all out o' shape.*

For two days now he'd been planting tobacco in the cold and wet, and still the rain kept falling. Every day the work was the same: He and the girl dug up seedlings from the bed by the house and took them into the fields, where Holt and Fanshawe rooted them, one to a hill. By now Holt could set as many as three plants a minute, Fanshawe rather less. It was all Rob and the girl could do to keep them supplied.

Gasping for breath, Rob set a bunch of seedlings down in the muddy row where Holt was hoeing. "Bring more next time, boy," Holt snapped. "And don't dawdle."

"Yes, sir."

Rob sloshed his way back to the tobacco bed, keeping an eye out for snakes. Hunter's Toyle had seemed desolate enough in good weather, but in this torrent it looked like the Devil's own acre. Water streamed down the fields, making rivers of the stumpy rows. Through the heavy curtain of rain Rob spied Master Freed and his son working on their own section of land on the other side of the palisade. Both had the hunched appearance of desperate men.

Rob, too, was feeling desperate. Life in London had been difficult, but nothing like as bad as this. He was finding it harder and harder to believe that Nell was still alive. Indeed, by now he was so benumbed by rain and mud that she kept slipping from his mind, along with all the rest of his memories.

Shivering wet, he knelt in the mud of the tobacco bed. *I'm as good as dead, slaving like this with no one to speak to. No one here even remembers me name.* With stiff hands he dug up a few more of the tender plants. *Better hurry,* he thought, *or Holt will be angry.*

A hand grabbed his soaking shirt and dragged him backward. When he tried to resist, a voice hissed in his ear. "Snake!"

Rob watched, wide-eyed, as the Indian girl leaped in front of him and hacked at the ground with a hoe. A moment later he was staring down at the tobacco bed, where a thick brown snake lay cloven in two, thrashing the muddy waters even in death.

Stunned, he looked up at the Indian girl. "You saved me." And then it hit him. "You spoke. You spoke *English.*"

She stared at him blankly, as if she didn't understand.

"I heard you," he insisted softly.

She turned her back on him and pushed the hoe into the dark, wet earth.

He couldn't let it go. "You said 'snake.'"

"Hush!" Her face was full of fear. "They hear."

So he was right! She could speak English.

He glanced down the field at Holt and Fanshawe. "They'll not hear us. They're too far away." Still he dropped his voice. "I'll not tell them you can speak, I swear."

Bent low over the tobacco, she gave no sign she was listening to him.

"What is your name?" he whispered.

She did not answer.

He asked the question again. "Please—what are you called?"

The answer was so soft, he almost missed it. "Mattoume."

He tried to repeat what he'd heard. "Ma-TOOM."

At last she faced him, her eyes dark and steady.

"I'm Rob. Rob Brackett."

"Rob," she repeated.

"Boy!" Holt's voice carried across the fields. "Where are you?"

"Coming, sir!" But first, Rob thought, he would ask Mattoume another question. Almost anything would do. Anything, he thought, to keep her talking. "How old are you?"

She hesitated. "Ten . . . and two."

"Twelve," he said.

"Boy!" Holt bellowed.

"Go," Mattoume urged.

"I'm thirteen," he told her. "Ten and three." His

arms full of seedlings, he ran back through the mud to Holt.

To speak with someone who did not own him—it seemed a miracle to Rob. So much of a miracle that he wondered if it had really happened. *Mayhap the work and weather has gone to me head. Mayhap it was only a dream.*

But when they next met at the tobacco bed, Mattoume whispered to him, "You look for girl?"

He stared at her. "What do you know about that?"

"You say at church. To old man."

Of course. On Sunday Mattoume had been standing right next to him when he'd talked to Sam Dobson. But back then he hadn't known she could understand what he was saying.

"She's called Nell," he explained. "Nell Cranston. She's younger than you—only nine years old. And she's a Londoner and an orphan, same as me."

He wasn't sure Mattoume would understand all that, but she nodded and asked, "Where Nell now?"

He grabbed hold of a seedling. "I don't know."

Mattoume looked at him directly, her eyes full of sorrow. "Lost?"

His throat tightened. "Yes." Gruffly he asked, "What o' your folks? Where are they?"

She gestured north. "Live by river. Five days' journey."

"Do you have sisters?" he asked. "Brothers?"

"Two sisters. Two brothers. Father is *cawcauwa-sough*," she said proudly.

"Co-co—" He tried to repeat the word she had said, then gave up. "What is that?"

She thought for a moment. "Is important man. Help *weroance*."

"*Weroance*," Rob echoed. The word felt strange on his tongue.

Mattoume explained that a *weroance* was the leader of a village or a group of villages. If the leader was a woman, she was called a *weroansqua*. As she spoke, Rob marveled at her command of English. He could understand her perfectly.

He was about to ask her how she'd learned the language so well when Mattoume rose from the tobacco bed, her hands full of tobacco shoots. "I go now. Talk later?"

"Talk later," he agreed, and watched her walk away through the rain.

Chapter 10

Over the next two days, in snatched moments and soft whispers, Rob and Mattoume talked whenever they could.

Mattoume explained that she'd learned English from her older brother, who had a gift for languages and often translated for the *weroance*. "Now I listen. Learn more." She nodded toward the end of the field, where Holt and Fanshawe stood digging. "They not know I understand." She glanced fiercely at Rob. "No one know. Is *secret*."

"I'll not tell them," Rob promised. "I already said as I wouldn't. Remember?"

The next time he met up with Mattoume at the tobacco bed, Rob asked, "What does Indian talk sound like?"

She frowned. "I not Indian. I Pamunkey."

"Then how does Pamunkey talk sound?"

She thought for a moment, then spoke a quick phrase full of strange sounds.

Rob tried to bend his mouth around the words. "It don't sound right when I say it," he said, discouraged.

Mattoume said the phrase more slowly, then coached him through it one syllable at a time. When he finally strung them all together, she smiled at him. "Good."

Rob was going to ask her what it meant when Holt called them out of the field and marched them back to the house. There they had no chance to talk.

All that evening Rob practiced the Pamunkey words in his head. The next morning he proudly repeated them to Mattoume while they were working in the tobacco bed. "What am I saying?" he asked.

She put her hand to her mouth. For a moment he wondered if he'd done something wrong. But no, she was simply hiding a smile. "You say, 'I stink like dead fish.'"

"What?" He was outraged. When she giggled, he turned away to hide his anger and embarrassment.

"Rob?"

He very nearly didn't answer her. "What?"

She sounded worried. "You not say, 'I stink like dead fish.'"

He wouldn't look at her. "Oh?"

"You say, 'I friend.'"

He glanced at her and saw an anxious look in her eyes. She really meant it, he realized. She wanted them to be friends.

He looked down at the muddy earth. *The first thing a friend does is rob you blind.* That's what he'd told Nell on board the *Sparrow*. And in his experience it was true.

Yet he didn't think Mattoume was trying to take advantage of him. True, she'd made a joke at his expense—but she had also saved his life. What better proof of friendship could he ask?

Guess she don't mean me no harm, he decided. Slowly he repeated the phrase she had taught him. "I friend," he said, stumbling over the Pamunkey words. "I friend."

When he looked up again, Mattoume was smiling.

As the afternoon wore on the rain grew lighter and lighter, till at last the clouds parted, revealing blue sky. By sunset only a few wisps of cloud remained.

"We'll not have rain on the morrow," Holt predicted. "But no matter. The transplanting is almost done."

"And a dashed good thing, too," Fanshawe muttered, his face slack with exhaustion. "We could do with a rest."

Rob doubted a rest was what Holt had in mind.

But he would be glad to leave off transplanting. Perhaps now he and Mattoume would be assigned to a task that would allow them to talk with each other more freely.

When darkness fell, Holt marched them all back to the house, where they shared a silent supper of leftover corn hash. Meager as it was, it appeared to lift Fanshawe's spirits. When the meal was over, he stuffed a clay pipe full of dried tobacco and bent to the dying fire. With a bit of kindling he lit the pipe, then returned to the table.

"We could do with a spot of entertainment after all that grubbing about," he said to Holt. "In fact, I think we deserve it. Shall we call upon Captain Morgan?"

"No," said Holt. "There's too much that needs doing on the morrow. The corn needs hoeing—"

"And we need money," said Fanshawe.

Holt raised an eyebrow. "What are you proposing?"

Fanshawe leaned across the table. "Why, to strike up a game, of course! You know no one can touch us at cards."

Holt shook his head. "There are laws against gaming here. You know that. We could lose all our winnings, and more."

"Captain Morgan won't give us away, cousin. Nor will his friends, if they join us."

"'Tis true we could use the money," Holt admitted.

He eyed Rob and Mattoume. "I suppose Hades could keep the two of them in check."

"And Morgan's place is but thirty yards distant," Fanshawe added in a wheedling tone.

Holt stared at Rob and Mattoume for a few moments more, then nodded. "All right. We'll do it. But we'll take our guns with us."

Rob kept his eyes on his trencher, afraid that if he so much as looked at Mattoume, Holt might suspect something was up. But as soon as the cousins were well away from the dwelling, he and Mattoume began to talk—in whispers only, to be sure of hearing Holt and Fanshawe when they returned.

Mattoume told him more about her family and her people, the Pamunkeys. Before long Rob was telling her about his father and about how he had dreamed of becoming a carpenter like him, though he now doubted that dream would ever come true.

"Carpenter," Mattoume repeated, squirreling the word away for future use. In the past two days she had learned more than two dozen words from Rob, which impressed him mightily. It was all he could do to remember the few Pamunkey phrases she'd taught him.

Sitting by the hearth, they shared stories of how they'd been captured. Rob's face burned as he recounted how he'd been gulled by Kit. When he fell silent, Mattoume explained that she had been kidnapped last summer, in the time she called *cohattayough*. She'd been gathering healing herbs for her grandmother when an English trader had taken her captive. "He tie me, take me away. Then sell me."

"To Holt?"

"No. To another master. He die in *cattapeuk*—spring. Then Holt buy me." She had been in Hunter's Toyle for only a month before Rob arrived, she explained.

"The Indians at church," Rob asked, "are they Pamunkey, too?"

"They are Accomacks, I think."

"Don't you know for sure?"

Mattoume shook her head. "They keep us apart."

When she spoke again, it was about her family. She missed them all, even her brother's sharp-tongued wife. Above all, she missed her grandmother and her little sisters. If she were home, she'd be helping them in the cornfields.

Corn was the Pamunkeys' most important crop, she told Rob, and it was the women of the village who tended it. Together they planted the corn and weeded it and sang prayers for a good harvest. In midsummer, when the early corn became ripe, the whole village celebrated together.

Lately, however, her people had done more grieving

than celebrating. Each summer, just before harvest, the English had attacked, setting fire to fields and villages and killing as many Pamunkeys as possible. Although her own village had been spared, refugees from other villages had come to them, seeking food and shelter. It was hard to feed everyone. "Many person hungry," Mattoume said. "Many baby cry."

Her words disturbed Rob. Casting about for a way to defend his countrymen, he said, "'Tis wrong, killing women and children. But your people've done as much to us English. Why, on the boat coming over here I heard as how five years ago you Pamunkeys killed four hundred settlers in one go."

"English kill first," said Mattoume, her voice flat and angry. "Kill many, many Pamunkey."

They sat in silence for some time. Then Mattoume leaned forward. "Is bad to kill. But English take corn and land, bring sickness, train dogs to attack us."

Again seeking to defend his countrymen, Rob seized on this last claim and said, "They train them? How do you know?"

This provoked a flurry of words from Mattoume, not all of which he could easily understand. But the gist of them was that the English used their dogs—especially mastiffs like Hades—to hunt down Pamunkeys and other Indians and to maul their children. Indeed, it was against Virginia law for an

English colonist to sell a mastiff or a gun to an Indian; both were considered valuable weapons.

"English destroy us," Mattoume finished. "Pamunkeys must fight—or die."

Rob stared at the dirt floor. He didn't know what to say. It was clear that his countrymen had done things he found shameful. If he had been born a Pamunkey, perhaps he, too, would have risen up against them. Yet it felt disloyal to say so.

To cover his confusion, he said, "What's it like, being raised Pamunkey?"

Softly Mattoume spoke of the baskets her grandmother had taught her to weave, of the sweet drink her aunts made from walnuts, of the bread they made from *mattoume,* the grass for which she'd been nicknamed. She told him, too, of the clothes she used to wear, made from soft deerskin, not the rough, dirty fabric she was forced to wear now. Finally, she spoke of her mother, who had died of fever three summers ago.

"I can't hardly remember me own ma," Rob admitted. "I was that small when she died. But me father told me about her. He said as I had her eyes and her smile."

"I look like father," Mattoume said.

"Why don't he come looking for you?" Rob wanted to know.

Mattoume stared at the banked coals in the fireplace. "I not know," she whispered. "Mayhap he is sick or wounded. Or he not know where to find me." She was near tears.

A moment later she squared her chin. "I go back soon. I run."

Rob rocked back on his heels. He couldn't believe it. Here he'd been thinking they were friends, and all along she'd been leading up to this. *Just another Kit she is,* he thought angrily, *playing me for a fool.*

"And you expect me to help you, is that it?" He didn't give her a chance to answer him. "Even though it means a flogging for me."

She shook her head impatiently. "Holt not flog you."

Rob snorted. Who did she think she was fooling? "He'll flog me, all right. Come close to killing me, I shouldn't wonder."

"He not flog you," Mattoume said, "if you come with me."

Chapter 11

Rob stared at Mattoume. He'd not expected any-thing like this. "You want me to run away with you?"

She nodded.

"But your people would kill me."

"Not kill you," Mattoume said. "Make you Pa-munkey."

"An English Pamunkey?" He almost laughed out loud. "A strange notion, that."

"Other English, they Pamunkey now."

Rob frowned, not understanding. "Other English?"

"Men and boys. Servants. They run away, join Pamunkeys."

"You make them serve you?"

She gave him an exasperated look. "Make them *brothers*. My cousin, Pemmenaw—she lose son. Now English boy her son. Is Pamunkey way."

Rob thought this over. Back in London he'd never have believed that Englishmen would ever willingly turn their backs on their own kind. Now, however, he saw things differently. *Them six servants as died here, they'd have been a sight better off running away than staying here with Holt,* he thought.

Still, his mind boggled at the idea. "I can't see living in a cave," he told Mattoume. "Nor eating such strange stuff as is out in the woods. And I won't eat other people, neither," he added quickly, remembering what he'd heard in Jamestown about Indians sometimes stooping to cannibalism.

Mattoume clicked her tongue indignantly. "We not eat people! And we not live in caves. We live in houses. Houses made with saplings, mats, and bark."

"Bark?" Rob said dubiously.

"Is good." Mattoume looked around the slipshod hut and wrinkled her nose. "Not like here."

Well, at least they could both agree that the huts in Hunter's Toyle were no prize. Yet Rob had his doubts that he'd find bark houses much to his liking, either. "You've no call for fine carpentry, have you?"

Mattoume hesitated. "No." But she urged him to come with her, saying that the life he would lead among the Pamunkeys was much better than anything he could expect from the English. With her people he could hunt and fish. He could play games to strengthen his skill with a bow and arrow. He could be part of her family.

It's nothing like the life I dreamed of back in London, Rob thought when she finished. *But I guess it'd be better than the one I has now.*

All the same, he was suspicious. "How do I know you're telling me the truth?"

She glared at him. "I not lie."

He persisted. "But you've been gone so long. How can you be sure your family will want me?"

"Is Pamunkey way," she said again. "You help me, they welcome you."

Rob found it hard to credit such generosity. "How do I know you'll not lose me in the woods somewhere and go on without me?"

"We go together," Mattoume said. "I promise."

She sounded as if she meant it. Yet even if her offer was genuine, could he really bring himself to accept it? Bleak as life was in English Virginia, there was much here that was familiar to him. The other settlers spoke his own language. They dressed as he did. They ate the same foods, knew the same songs. *I'll lose all that if I goes with Mattoume,* he thought.

"Rob?" Though Mattoume was comfortable with long pauses, from the sound of her voice this one had gone on too long.

Not sure what to say next, he stayed silent—and

heard the clink of Hades's chain and the thump of boots approaching the door.

Holt and Fanshawe were coming back. Rob rose in a panic. If the cousins found their two servants awake by the hearth, they might suspect a conspiracy.

"Quick!" he whispered to Mattoume. "Up the ladder!"

But Mattoume was ahead of him. Already she had darted to the ladder and was climbing up it. As Rob waited below, the door burst open.

"A fine evening, cousin," declared Fanshawe, "and—"

Rob grabbed hold of the ladder, but it was too late. Holt was striding toward him, musket in hand.

"What are you doing up, boy?"

"I—er—I woke and heard someone coming." In a burst of inspiration, Rob added, "I thought as how it might be Indians, sir."

Holt cuffed him. "Don't lie to me, boy!"

Rob gulped. How did Holt know he was lying? Had he overheard them? Or had he just guessed?

"You're after the supper leavings," Holt went on, cuffing Rob again. "Just for that, you'll miss breakfast, you thieving brat. Now up to the loft with you—and be quick about it!"

As Rob scampered up the ladder, Holt swatted his backside with the musket. Rob nearly fell off the ladder from the force of the blow.

Angry and sore, he hoisted himself into the loft and

lay down on his belly beside Mattoume. He heard Holt and Fanshawe down below, swigging a bottle of spirits and crowing over their takings from the card game. Even from the loft he could smell the stink of tobacco smoke on them.

He stared wide-eyed into the darkness. It was true that if he stayed here in Hunter's Toyle, he'd be among people who spoke his language and understood his ways. Yet what did such similarities mean, in the end? Did he really want to share anything with the likes of Holt and Fanshawe? Did he really want to claim them as his own kind? And even if he did, what then? *They'd still treat Hades more decent than they treat me,* he thought.

He glanced at Mattoume, barely visible beside him in the shadowy loft. If he felt kinship with anyone here in Virginia, it was with her. She had saved his life. She was his friend if anyone was.

Don't trust no one. That's what he'd told Nell back in London. And he didn't find it easy to trust Mattoume now, still less her family, whom he had never seen. But there was another piece of advice he'd given to Nell: *Look out for yourself.* And right now it seemed that the best way he could look after himself was to run away with Mattoume. After all, if he stayed here in Hunter's Toyle, he'd likely not survive the year.

The cousins were still talking below. Slowly, soundlessly, Rob tilted his head toward Mattoume. "All right," he whispered. "We go together."

The following night, when Holt and Fanshawe again went to Captain Morgan's to play cards, Rob and Mattoume planned their escape. They would need food, but since Mattoume was in charge of the cooking, that seemed no great obstacle, especially since they would be able to supplement their fare by foraging in the woods for berries and greens.

Rob couldn't help thinking of what else they might find in the woods. "I know you has ways of dealing with snakes," he said. "But what about wolves and bears?"

"Walk in stream, wolves not smell us," Mattoume said.

"What stream?" Rob hoped she didn't mean the creek that ran past Hunter's Toyle. It was awfully deep for wading, and parts of it lay within sight of the palisade.

"Stream in woods," Mattoume said. "I show you." She began drawing a rough map in the cold ashes by the hearth. She'd seen the stream twice, she explained, once when she'd been brought to Hunter's Toyle and once when Fanshawe had gone out hunting and taken her to carry the game back. Holt had been off in Jamestown that day, but Hades had been with them, or else she would have tried to run then.

"How far does this stream run?" Rob asked, looking down at the map.

"Far enough." They would follow it as long as they could, she said, so that Hades wouldn't pick up their scent. After that they'd just have to do the best they could.

"What if we get lost?" he asked uneasily.

"I follow river, see stars," she said. "We find way again."

She sounded confident, but Rob remained worried. "What about the bears?"

"Bears not much trouble."

Rob rolled his eyes.

"Is true," she insisted. "English run—bear chase them. Pamunkey stay still—bear go away."

"Always?"

She shrugged. "Most times."

Rob did not find this completely reassuring. But given the choice between a bear and Holt, he decided he'd take his chances with the bear.

If it hadn't been for Hades, Rob and Mattoume might have tried to escape that very night. But whenever they stopped whispering, they heard the mastiff pacing just outside the door. While he stood guard, they would never get away.

Mattoume told Rob that Hades had foiled her previous attempts to run away, both of which had taken place before his arrival. One night she'd tried to escape from the hut, only to be cornered by Hades the moment she crossed the threshold. He'd caught her, too, the one time she'd tried to edge out of the tobacco field without anyone seeing.

"What if we fed him some scraps?" Rob asked. "Mayhap he'd be friends with us then."

"I already try," Mattoume said. "He stay mean."

"Won't do no harm to try again," Rob said.

They started their campaign the next morning. When Holt and Fanshawe weren't looking, Mattoume threw the mastiff a bit of her breakfast. Rob tossed him small scraps of bone.

Hades wolfed down their gifts but continued to snap at them every time they passed by.

"'Tis no use," said Rob after a week had gone by. "He hates us, he does."

Since bribery hadn't worked, they tried poison. While fetching water from the creek, Rob gathered some evil-looking berries that Mattoume had warned him not to eat. Back at the house he smeared them on a bit of meat and threw it to Hades. The dog sniffed at the meat, then stalked away. After that he would eat nothing but what came from Holt's own hand.

May passed into June, and Rob grew discouraged. How would he and Mattoume ever find a chance to escape? Holt worked them like oxen every waking hour, except on Sundays, when they were required to be at church. Though he and Mattoume had hoped the journeys to Jamestown might give them the opportunity to run, none had so far appeared.

He was grateful for Sundays all the same, not only because they offered him a brief respite from field work, but also because they allowed him the chance to ask other servants if they had seen Nell. Unfortunately, however, no one had. Some nights Rob found it hard to sleep, so worried was he over what had become of the girl.

Most of the time, however, he was weary from the day's work and fell asleep as soon as he reached the loft. Holt was working them so hard that Rob was exhausted all the time—and hungry, too, as hungry as he had been on the worst days back in London's alleys. But their supplies were low and the garden was slow to ripen, so every day Rob went starving into the fields, and every day the work seemed harder than ever.

And that was before the fever struck.

Master Freed's son succumbed to the contagion first. The next day Freed himself fell ill. Afraid that he, too, would catch the disease, Captain Morgan fled to friends in another settlement, while Holt warned his own household to keep their distance. "I'll not stick my neck out to help another planter," he told them, "not when I have my own fortune to make."

It took Rob aback to hear his own words on Holt's lips: *I'll not stick me neck out. . . .*

It don't mean nothing, Rob told himself firmly. Still, it unsettled him to find that he had anything in common with Holt, even if it was only words.

Two days later, Rob woke with a bad headache. Was it the fever? The thought filled him with dread. But when he felt his cheeks and forehead, he was relieved to find them no warmer than usual.

"Boy?" Holt bellowed. "Get down here!"

Rob stumbled down the ladder and joined the others in a meager breakfast. After the meal was over, Mattoume silently carried the cask of corn to the table and set it in front of Holt.

"Near empty, by God!" Holt glared at Mattoume, who had prudently stepped out of reach. "Why didn't you say—" With an oath, he cut off the question. "You cursed mute."

Fanshawe had rolled the empty cask across the table and was now staring into it. "We're going to starve."

Holt grabbed his musket. "God's blood, cousin, but you talk like a puling child. There's sure to be more grain in Jamestown. And we'll never starve so long as we can hunt."

Fanshawe brightened. "Hunting? This morn?"

"I'll take Hades with me," Holt decided. "You stay here, cousin, and see to the tobacco."

"That's not fair!" Fanshawe protested. "You can't leave me to do all the work!"

Holt fingered his musket. "I've done my share and more, cousin. And I say you will stay here." Though he spoke softly, there was menace in the words.

Fanshawe slumped back in his chair. As Holt and Hades left the paling, he murmured, "He'd never have dared give me orders in England. Never!" Then he caught sight of Rob. "What are you looking at, boy?"

"Nothing, sir," Rob said.

In truth, he'd been thinking that with Holt and Hades gone, they might finally have an opportunity to run. He reckoned Mattoume was thinking along the same lines. She'd disappeared into the loft as Holt was leaving, and Rob guessed she was retrieving the store of dried corn and berries they'd been saving for their escape. They had stowed the food under the straw that served as their bed, in a small linen bag that one of the dead servants had left behind. Mattoume was planning to wear the bag under her skirt, hidden among its voluminous folds.

"Fetch your hoe, boy," Fanshawe told him. "We've work to do. Where's that blasted girl?"

By the time he finished speaking, Mattoume was already halfway down the ladder. Together they headed toward the fields. At first Rob didn't dare to look at Mattoume, for fear he would give something away. But when Fanshawe wasn't looking, Mattoume caught Rob's eye and patted the side of her skirt. She had the bag of food.

Fanshawe noticed nothing. Indeed, he hardly seemed to look at either of them during the first hour they worked. Then, as the sun rose still higher, he set down his hoe.

"It's time I had a brief rest." He spoke defiantly, as if half expecting someone to argue with him. "You watch that Indian while I'm gone, boy. Do you understand me?"

"Yes, sir."

Fanshawe ambled down to the creek. Head reeling with the heat, Rob exchanged a sidelong glance with Mattoume. Was this their chance?

"Wait," Mattoume mouthed.

Rob nodded. The creek was in clear sight of the fields, so if all Fanshawe had in mind was a quick drink, there would be no time to run away. But Fanshawe had said he wanted a rest. Perhaps he would set himself down by the creek for a while. Perhaps he would even fall asleep. Rob's heart beat faster in anticipation.

For the next several minutes, he and Mattoume chopped steadily at the weeds with their hoes. Every so often they looked up from the ground and glanced at each other and then at Fanshawe. He was kneeling by the creek now, splashing water over his face and hands.

A splash of cold water would feel good, Rob thought as he laid into the next hill of tobacco. He was so dizzy with heat, he could hardly stay upright. When Mattoume nudged him, he nearly toppled over.

"Look," she whispered, her dark cheeks flushed with excitement.

Rob steadied himself with the hoe and squinted back at Fanshawe. But the sun seemed to shine in his eyes, and when he blinked, the world set to spinning again.

"He sleep," Mattoume said.

"How can you tell?" Rob asked weakly.

"I wave hoe," she said. "He not move."

She waved it again, high over her head. Fanshawe remained quite still.

She laid the hoe down on the ground. "We go," she urged.

Rob nodded and set down his own hoe. Without its support, however, he found it hard to stand. He stared at the ground, trying to steady himself, then glanced up at Mattoume. She was already some distance ahead of him. He took a step after her—and fell to his knees.

He tried to rise, but the sun weighed him down, burning his body, branding his brain. He buried his face in his hands.

"Rob!" It was Mattoume, kneeling down beside him. She put her hand against his cheek, then said a word in her own tongue, a word he could not understand. "Fever," she translated. "You have fever."

'Tisn't the fever, he tried to say. *'Tis the sun what's holding me down. Can't you see it coming closer and closer?* But his swollen tongue wouldn't form the words.

"Rob?"

He did not hear her. He only saw the sun, so blinding white it blotted out everything else.

Chapter 12

For seven days Rob burned with fever. When at last it released him, he was too weak to move. Hour after hour he lay stretched out on a pallet in front of the hearth. Beside him lay Mattoume, who was also gravely ill.

She could have run, he thought. *She could have left me on that there field and saved herself.*

Instead, she'd stood by him. She'd helped Fanshawe carry him back to the house, and she'd nursed him until she herself had fallen ill. That much he remembered.

He knew, none better, that loyalty like that was rare. And now Mattoume was paying the price for it.

He turned his head toward the pallet where she was lying. Her walnut skin was red-hot now, and her black hair was matted against her head. Rob listened to the breath rasping in her throat. What would he do if she died?

For the first time since his father's death, a prayer welled up inside him. *Let her live. Please let her live.*

In a distant corner of the room Fanshawe moaned, for he, too, had succumbed to the sickness. Of them all, only Holt remained untouched.

He would, thought Rob bitterly. But at least Holt had not turned his back on them. Though he cursed them by night and by day, he also brought them water and fed them thin gruel. Now he came in the door, bearing water from the creek.

"I'll not have you die on me," he said, forcing the water down Mattoume's throat. "I've lost enough servants to fever already."

Mattoume moaned.

Holt's eyes narrowed. "So you've a voice after all, eh?"

Rob lay very still. Struck senseless by the fever, Mattoume might very well blurt out something in English. She might even speak of their plans to run away. And what would happen then? *We've already missed one chance to escape,* Rob thought. *If Holt catches on to us, we'll never get another.*

But for now, at least, Mattoume spoke no words at all, not even Pamunkey ones. She only moaned, and very softly at that.

"Stupid girl," said Holt, and he went to give Fanshawe his share of the water.

Lying cold and helpless beside Mattoume, Rob prayed again for her recovery. And then he added a prayer that she be silent, too—at least when Holt was around.

A week later the fever passed from Mattoume. In all that time she spoke no more than a few hoarse Pamunkey words that no one heard except Rob. And one day after that Fanshawe's fever broke, too, leaving him weak and fretful but nevertheless alive. The others who lived in Hunter's Toyle had not fared so well, Rob learned. Captain Morgan had survived, but both the Freeds had perished.

Holt laid claim to the Freeds' fields, boat, and barrel of corn. To be sure, the fields were only his until the court could sort out the Freeds' estate. But since they had died without a will and without relatives in Virginia, it would be a long time, perhaps years, before the matter was settled. In the meantime, Holt told Fanshawe, they needn't be too careful in keeping accounts. Indeed, when they harvested tobacco this fall, they might as well count most of the Freeds' crop as their own, for no one was likely to challenge them. As for the boat and the barrel of corn, Holt planned to tell the court the Freeds had sold it to him before they died. "No great loss without some small gain," he said, his eyes bright with satisfaction.

By then Rob was hobbling around the hearth, tending Mattoume and Fanshawe while Holt worked the fields. The next day Holt pressed a hoe into his hand and sent him outdoors.

Rob soon discovered he had not yet reached his full strength. Though his fear of Holt made him work hard, he could not stoop without feeling dizzy. Nor could he weed more than a dozen hills of tobacco before needing a rest. Holt swore at him, then sent him back to the house. "You're of no use to me, boy."

In time, however, Rob recovered fully from the fever. So did Fanshawe and Mattoume. By mid-July they were all out in the fields again, weeding the tobacco plants and checking for worms. Rob's muscles ached from all the stooping and hoeing. More often than not his belly growled, too. The Freeds' corn barrel was running low, and meals were growing scanty.

"'Tis time I hired you out, boy," Holt announced one evening.

Fanshawe looked up from his supper. "What are you talking about, cousin? We need him in the fields."

"Not as badly as we need corn. Best we hire the boy out and buy more corn with what he brings us."

Fanshawe frowned. "Has anyone made an offer for his time?"

"Not yet. But I'll find someone to take him, never

fear." Holt turned to Rob again. "We go to Jamestown on the morrow, boy."

Rob was careful not to glance at Mattoume. Although they were still planning to run away, they hadn't had much chance lately to discuss their plans. Now, under Holt's watchful eye, he dared not even look at her.

By the time Rob and Mattoume were settled in the loft, however, Holt and Fanshawe were too busy arguing over what to buy with Rob's wages to overhear any whispers above them.

Rob folded his knees against his chest. "Looks like I'll be gone for a week, mayhap more."

Mattoume was silent. In the darkness he could barely see her.

"You won't—" He hesitated. "You won't run away without me, will you?"

"No," said Mattoume. "We go *together*."

Rob was relieved to hear it. "Together," he agreed. "Just as soon as we can."

The next morning Holt and Rob traveled down to Jamestown on the boat that Holt had taken for his own after the Freeds died.

"Morgan says a ship's come in and has passed its quarantine, so the place should be busier than usual," Holt had told his cousin before they left. "I'll get a good price for the boy there."

Jamestown was indeed very busy. Dozens of men milled about the church. A crowd had gathered at the landing, waving to the passengers on the ship anchored offshore.

Rob couldn't help staring at the ship. It was a link to his old life, to London, to England. How far he had come! Nor was he done with traveling yet, for if the ocean that separated London and Virginia was wide, the gulf that separated Englishmen and Pamunkeys was still wider. And that was the gulf he would have to cross when he ran away with Mattoume.

"You're lagging behind, boy!"

Rob winced as Holt grabbed his shoulder and forced him down the street.

They stopped first at a storehouse, where Holt set an empty cask before the beefy trader. "I want this filled with corn."

The trader crossed his arms over his chest. "Let me see your money first."

"Oh, you'll be paid, my good man. Never fear." Holt pushed Rob forward. "I've a carpenter's boy here that I'm looking to hire out. Where will I get the best price for him?"

The trader looked at Rob. "This is the boy?"

"Yes. A master craftsman, despite his youth."

Rob nearly rolled his eyes but stopped himself in time. *But won't Mattoume laugh when I tells her,* he thought.

The trader tugged thoughtfully at his spattered apron. "You might talk to Tom Stanton. He's the carpenter over by Hog Island, on the other side of the river. I know he's looking for a boy."

Stanton. The name sounded familiar to Rob. But why?

Holt frowned at the trader. "Across the river, you say? I've no time for that."

"You're in luck, then. Stanton was in here not half an hour ago, buying corn. Said he was expecting a shipment of tools on the ship that's lying in the harbor, and he'd not go back across the river till he had them in his hands. If you make haste, you'll likely find him down by the landing."

Thinking back, Rob at last remembered where he had heard the name Stanton before. *The man as spoke to me about carpentry back when they was a-selling us off,* he thought, *his name was Stanton.* Was it the same man?

"Will he pay a good price for the boy?" asked Holt.

"I daresay he will. He's made a pretty penny in Virginia, old Tom has. And he's been wanting a boy for weeks now."

Holt nodded. "He's the man for me, then." He prodded Rob toward the door. "Come along, boy. Let's see what kind of money this Stanton will offer for a fortnight of your time."

Chapter 13

They found Tom Stanton down by the landing, prying open a long, flat box. He was the same man whom Rob had been thinking of, the one who'd spoken to him on the day he'd been sold. A strong man and a stocky one, with callused hands and kind brown eyes.

"I've an offer to put to you," Holt said to him after the introductions were over.

"Wait a moment," said Stanton.

Holt started to object, then fell silent. It seemed he had decided a quarrel was not in his best interest.

Stanton pulled the lid off the box. There, in a bed of sawdust, lay the first smoothing plane Rob had seen since his father's shop had burned down. Stanton pulled the plane out of the box, flipped it over, and examined the underside. Then he glanced up at Rob with a ghost of a smile in his eyes.

He remembers me, Rob thought.

Stanton flipped the plane back over and settled it into the box. Then he stood up. "What can I do for you?" he asked Holt.

"I heard you were looking for a boy."

"A skilled one," said Stanton.

"He's as skilled as they come," said Holt, pushing Rob forward. "What is he worth to you?"

"You're looking to sell him?"

"Not sell him—hire him out."

"For how long?"

"A week or so," said Holt. "Are you interested?"

"I might be." Stanton turned to Rob and nodded toward the box that lay in the sand. "Can you tell me what that is?"

Rob seized the chance to prove himself. "A plane, sir. A smoothing plane."

"And what is it used for?"

"To smooth a board after the jack plane's been over it, sir."

Stanton nodded. "Pick it up."

Rob hoisted it out of the box.

"Show me how you hold it," Stanton said.

Before he had finished speaking, Rob's hands had already angled themselves around the tool. It felt good to have a plane in his hands again. So good, in fact, that he forgot he was being tested and said, "'Tis a fine piece, sir. Me father—"

Holt cuffed him. "Enough, boy."

Stanton went very still for a moment, then took the tool from Rob. "It is indeed a fine piece. I'm pleased you see that." He laid the plane back in the box and turned to Holt. "I'll take the lad for the week, or even longer if you can spare him. And I'll pay you three shillings a day."

"Four," said Holt.

"Three."

"Four," Holt repeated. "And you'll bring the boy back to Jamestown. I can't afford to waste a day crossing the river to fetch him back."

"I'll bring the boy back to Jamestown, but I'll not pay you a penny more than three shillings a day."

"Four."

"Three. But I'll pay you in advance."

Holt considered this. "In advance, you say?"

Stanton nodded.

Holt's eyes glinted. "Today?"

"Aye."

"Done." Holt thrust Rob toward the carpenter. "You can have him for a full fortnight, so long as you pay me now."

Within the hour Rob was crossing the James River in a strange craft called a canoe. Mattoume had told him about such boats, each one made from a hollowed-out log. Light and narrow, they bobbed lightly on the surface of the river. Fearful of falling out, Rob took pains to sit very still.

From behind him came the swish of Stanton's paddle cutting through the river. So far Stanton hadn't said much to him, perhaps because there'd been so much business to take care of. It had taken a while to find witnesses to the agreement, and after that was settled, Stanton had to go searching for the neighbor who'd crossed the river with him, a young man named Naylor.

Like Stanton, Naylor was a quiet man and a good paddler. It wasn't long before they were passing Hog Island.

"We don't live on the island itself," Stanton told Rob. "We live just south of it." He pointed. "'Tis the settlement up there on the shore. Parr's Hundred is its name."

Rob craned his neck, but the bluff was too high for him to see anything but a few rooftops.

When the canoe caught on the river-bottom, the men leaped out and waded through the shallows, pulling the boat behind them. Rob helped them drag the canoe to the landing place, some two hundred yards from the palisade, where two canoes and a flat-bottomed boat lay beached in the sun.

Naylor grinned at Rob. "Good work, lad." Still

grinning, he turned to Stanton. "How much did you pay for him?"

"Three shillings a day. And between us, I'd have been willing to pay more."

"More?" Naylor looked at Rob in surprise. "No offense, lad, but you're only half-grown."

"He's worth every penny," said Stanton. "You'll see why in a bit."

"What is it you do, lad?" Naylor joked. "Turn trees into houses in the space of a night?"

Rob didn't know what to say. He hadn't led Stanton to expect miracles from him, had he? "Sir, I'll do me best, but I'm only—"

"Hush, lad." Stanton spoke kindly. "I know what I'm about. And you will, too, soon enough." He handed Rob the box that contained the smoothing plane. "Carry this for me, lad. I'll take the others."

They proceeded up the broad path that led to the settlement, Rob with his one box, Stanton with two more, and Naylor with the canoe paddles in his arms.

"Will you dine with us, Naylor?" Stanton asked as they came up to the palisade.

Naylor steadied the paddles against his shoulder. "I shouldn't like to put Mistress Stanton to any trouble—"

"'Tis no trouble. Come."

As Rob followed them through the palisade gate

and down the path that ran through the settlement, he counted nearly two dozen snug houses, some with fenced-in yards for cattle and chickens. Every house save one had a garden, with neat rows of greens and cabbages and corn. In one garden Rob even saw bright yellow flowers.

It was nothing like London, of course. But Rob's standards had come down considerably since he'd reached Virginia. This settlement was small, but he liked the look of it.

O' course, it don't matter what I thinks of the place, he reminded himself quickly. *I'm just trading one master for another—and only for a fortnight, at that.*

Still, he couldn't deny that Stanton looked to be a much easier master than Holt. It would be a pleasure to work at his side and learn from him. Not that the learning would do him much good once he ran away with Mattoume. She'd told him her people didn't have much use for English carpentry. But that couldn't be helped.

Stanton nodded to two men talking over a fence and waved to a woman working in her garden. "Found yourself a new servant, then?" she asked, staring curiously at Rob.

"Indeed, I have," Stanton replied. He did not stop to elaborate but continued on down the row till they reached a long house with a well-shingled roof. Stanton turned into the yard and put his boxes down by the front door. "Set yours on top, lad. We'll tend to them in a moment."

As Rob set the box gently on top of the others, four small children raced around the corner of the house. A young girl followed behind them. "Kate, don't run so fast. You'll leave Daniel—" She caught sight of Rob and froze.

Rob's breath caught in his throat.

The girl ran across the yard and flung herself into his arms. "Rob!"

It was Nell.

Chapter 14

Nell, alive and safe. Who would have thought it? And yet here she was, as real as could be. Rob hugged her hard, lifting her off the ground. "Never thought I'd see you again, lass."

Recollecting he was among strangers, he blushed and set her down. *I must look a right gudgeon, going all softhearted like that.* But when he glanced at the gathering crowd, everyone was smiling at him in a welcoming way.

"So that was your secret, was it, Stanton?" said Naylor. "'Worth every penny,' you said. And you were right. It was."

"Let me introduce you to my family, lad," Stanton said. "These chicks"—he nodded toward two of the children next to Nell, a young girl and an even younger boy—"are named Kate and Daniel. And this is my wife, and our baby, Bess."

Mistress Stanton, a plain woman in a neat cap and blue dress, smiled and stepped forward to greet him, the baby in her arms. "Welcome, Rob Brackett. Young Nell hasn't stopped talking about you since the day she came here."

"Is she your servant, then?" Rob asked.

"No, she's ours," said a sallow woman on his right. "Master Stanton was kind enough to hire her for us, since he knew we'd been looking for such a girl to help me with the children and the cow and the garden. Of course, we repaid him as soon as he brought her here. My husband wouldn't hear of anything else." In a querulous voice, she added, "She's a bit younger than we had wanted, but she's a quick stepper, I'll give her that."

"This is Mistress Edgehill," Stanton said to Rob.

"And this is Master Henry Edgehill," said Nell, bending down toward one of the small boys at her side. "And Nicholas, his brother."

Rob nodded his head to acknowledge the introductions. To judge from the tone of her voice, Nell's mistress was not a warm-hearted woman, but Nell herself looked clean and well cared for, and she was smiling at the children as if she enjoyed their company. It seemed she'd fallen on her feet here in Parr's Hundred. Rob only wished he himself had done the same.

Apparently Stanton was thinking along the same lines. "I was sorry to lose you that day in Jamestown, lad. And I was sorrier still when I heard what young Nell had to say about you. Indeed, I was half tempted to go to your master and make an offer for you."

"You would've been asking for trouble if you had," Naylor said. "Captain Holt's known to be touchy about such matters." To Rob, he explained, "Last summer a man offered to buy one of your master's servants, but Holt misunderstood and thought the man was trying to take advantage of him. When they started to argue, Holt knocked him to the ground and scarred him for life. An ill-tempered man, your master."

"Indeed," Stanton said. "That is why I devised another plan. Rather than go after Captain Holt, I did my best to make him come after me."

Naylor grinned. "You do beat all, Stanton. Tell us, how did you manage it?"

Stanton's brown eyes twinkled. "I'd heard from a friend in Jamestown that Captain Holt was short of money. So I let it be known that I was looking for a skilled apprentice of, say, thirteen years of age—and that I would pay good money for one. Which was no more than the truth. And who should approach me today but Captain Holt himself."

"And now Rob's come to live in Parr's Hundred," Nell finished.

"No," Rob said quickly. "I'm here for a fortnight, that's all."

Nell's voice trembled. "But I thought . . ."

Mistress Edgehill frowned. "You should be thanking Master Stanton, Nell," she reprimanded. "'Tis a great favor he has done for your friend."

Bowing her head, Nell dutifully said her thanks.

"I wish it were more, lass," said Stanton. "But it cannot be helped. Now, come to the table, all of you, and let us dine together. Mistress Edgehill, I take it you will join us?"

As everyone surged toward the house, Rob and Nell hung back. "These here Edgehills—are they treating you well?" he asked.

"Oh, yes," she said quickly. "Of course, they keep me very busy, but I don't mind. The boys are very sweet."

"And their ma?"

Nell glanced uneasily toward the house. "She speaks very sharply sometimes, but I don't think she means to be unkind. She's upset this week because Master Edgehill is working upriver; he's a blacksmith by trade."

"She don't beat you?"

She shook her head. "Never." She looked up at him anxiously. "I've been worried about you, though. I keep thinking about that horrid man who bought you. . . ."

He's even worse than you imagine, Rob wanted to say. But what purpose would that serve, except to upset Nell?

"Don't you be worrying your head about me," he told her. "I can look after meself."

"Nell?" Mistress Edgehill called from inside the house. "Where are you? Come help me settle the boys."

Nell darted forward to help with her charges. Behind her Rob stopped awkwardly in the doorway. The Stantons' house was simple—just one long room and a loft—but it was far more spacious than the makeshift shelters in Hunter's Toyle, and much more carefully constructed. The plank floor, the solid shutters, the heavy chests: all spoke of a life Rob had thought he'd left far behind him.

"Come to the table, Rob," Mistress Stanton said warmly.

In most houses, Rob knew, he would have been expected to stand. Chairs weren't so common that every servant boy could have one. But this was a carpenter's house, with benches in plenty. Rob crossed over to the table and sat down beside Nell.

It was a long time since he had eaten at a table, longer still since he had eaten with a family about him. As he listened to Master Stanton say grace and watched Mistress Stanton serve the stew of duck and greens, he thought wistfully of his own parents. What would his life be like now if they had lived?

As everyone else began to eat, he tucked into his own trencher, which was twice as full as any he'd ever received in Hunter's Toyle. Beside him young Daniel dunked his spoon, handle and all, into his stew.

Mistress Stanton sighed. "Rob, would you—?"

Rob was already fishing out the spoon. Daniel looked on with round eyes. Around them conversation flowed freely as Stanton shared the news from Jamestown with his wife and Mistress Edgehill.

When everything noteworthy had been related, Naylor turned to Rob. "Do you know anything of our settlement, lad?"

"Next to nothing, sir. But it looks a fair place."

"It is, indeed," said Stanton. "Nearly seventy of us now dwell within its paling. We have our own storehouse—and even our own minister, as of this spring."

"And a good thing, too," added Naylor, "for we haven't enough boats to ferry us all to Jamestown of a Sunday."

"What is it like where you live, Rob?" Nell asked.

What could he say about his life that would not trouble her? "We live farther from the river than you do. And our trees are summat taller."

"Are there many people?"

He didn't want to talk about the people. "Not near so many as live here."

"Does your master own any other servants?"

"One."

"Another boy?"

"A girl," said Rob.

"From London?" Nell asked.

"No," said Rob. "She's an Indian."

Nell's eyes widened. "You live with an Indian?"

"Yes."

A short silence followed, broken only by Daniel's slurping.

Rob glanced around the table. The mere mention of an Indian had clearly taken them all aback. What would they say if they knew he was friends with the girl? That he could speak some Pamunkey? That he was planning to run away with her?

He stared at his empty plate. Best keep such facts to himself.

"Is she a Christian?" asked Mistress Edgehill.

"No. She don't even speak English." As soon as the lie was out of Rob's mouth, he wondered why he had told it. To protect Mattoume? Or to protect himself?

"I've seen Indians," young Nicholas Edgehill said. "They come here to trade."

"'Twould be better if they stayed away," Naylor said sharply.

"Now, you know the Accomacks who trade with us have always been peaceful," Master Stanton began.

Naylor's face was tight and closed. "They are still savages."

For a moment, no one said anything.

"How old is the girl?" Mistress Stanton asked Rob.

Rob shrugged. Perhaps if he gave only vague answers, they would stop asking questions. "Younger than me, I reckon."

"Sold by her parents, most likely," said Naylor.

Rob couldn't let this go by. "I heard as she was captured."

Stanton shook his head. "'Twould be better if we left such children alone."

"So you say," said Naylor. "But I say we need servants, and we may as well find them among the savages as elsewhere."

"I cannot agree," said Stanton. "It grieves their parents greatly, and leads them to war against us. And so it seems neither wise nor just—"

"Just?!" Naylor pushed away his plate. "What justice was there at Berkeley Hundred five years ago? Tell me that! Ten of my companions were foully murdered there, and twenty-two more at the captain's plantation. Good men and women, who died in agony, with—"

"Hush, man." Stanton's face was stern. "There are children here."

Naylor said nothing more, except to briefly beg pardon of Mistress Stanton and Mistress Edgehill. His mouth, however, remained tight with pain and anger.

"I have not forgotten that day, nor ever will," Stanton said quietly. "'Twas terrible beyond imagining. I grieve still for those who were lost."

Naylor's face eased a trifle.

"And I know 'tis true, what you say," Stanton went on. "The Indians will war against us whether we take their children or no. But—"

"They want to drive us from Virginia," Naylor interrupted. "But they will not succeed. They *must* not. For where else can we humble folk go? The rich ones among us have estates in England, but we do not. They do not even have work for us there anymore. Our homes, our families, our fortunes—all lie in Virginia now."

"We must endure," Stanton agreed, "or we will lose everything. But I still say it would be better if we did not force Indian children to serve us."

Naylor looked as if he were going to argue the point, but just then Daniel tossed his trencher to the floor with a triumphant shout, waking the baby in the cradle. Her cries brought the conversation to an end.

Glad of the diversion, Rob thought over all that he had just heard. *One thing's certain. I was right not to tell them Mattoume was me friend. Doubt even Master Stanton'd approve of that.*

"An excellent meal, Mistress Stanton," said Naylor. "Now I must take my leave of you, for I have much work to do this day."

"As have I." Stanton pushed his chair from the table and clasped his neighbor's hand. "Go safely, friend." As Naylor made his way out, Stanton smiled down at Rob. "Come, lad, let me show you the shop."

The shop!

Rob rose from his chair and followed Stanton out of the room.

Chapter 15

Stanton's shop lay under the same roof as the house, in an annex around back, its wide doors open to the yard outside.

'Tis smaller than me father's place, Rob thought. *And a sight newer, too.*

Yet there was much about the shop that was achingly familiar to him: the hammers and chisels, the golden-brown boards, the sweet smell of sawdust. Standing there, Rob felt as if he had found his way home.

Stanton began unpacking the boxes of tools he had brought back from Jamestown. "Nell says your father was a carpenter by trade, lad."

"Yes, sir."

"And you yourself have training in fine carpentry?"

"Yes, sir."

Stanton looked up from his workbench and smiled at Rob. "Of all my apprentices here in Virginia, you're the first who has known anything about fine carpentry. Four I've had, in all. One has already served his term, and two, alas, have died. But the other man is still with me. Wilkins is his name."

Rob had not realized he would be working with anyone but Stanton. "Will I be meeting him soon, sir?"

"Tomorrow, I expect," said Stanton. "Today he's working upriver, framing a house. He's a fine man, Wilkins, but only a middling carpenter. By which I mean his fences are better than his furniture. 'Twill be good to have you here to help with the finer work. Though it may be a good deal simpler than what you're used to. There's not much call for fancy carving and fretwork here in Virginia. Plain stuff, built well—that's what most folks want."

Rob was sorry to hear it. His fingers were itching to pick up Stanton's chisels and start carving. Still, to work with wood at all would be a pleasure.

"That said, now and again I do get a commission for something out of the ordinary," Stanton continued. "Why, just last week Sir Lionel Biggsby asked me to build him a cupboard, a present for his new wife. He wants something quite grand, he does. Mayhap you'll be able to help with that." He lifted a trying plane from the bench in front of him. "First, though, these boards need truing. Would you be up to the job?"

Rob took the long plane into his hands. "I hope so, sir."

Stanton led him over to the boards. "See what you can do with them, lad."

Rob picked up the first two boards and braced them in the bench, which stood by the open doors. Truing a board meant making sure it ran evenly, with straight edges that ensured a smooth join with the others. The task required concentration on Rob's part—concentration and steady hands and a good eye. Hard work, and yet Rob loved every moment of it. As he drew the long, heavy plane down the length of the first board, the misery of the past year dropped away from him. To work with wood again was a joy.

When Rob had finished with the boards, Stanton came over to see what kind of job he had done. After checking everything carefully, he said, "Your father taught you well."

No praise could have pleased Rob more. "He had a fine hand with wood, sir."

"I believe you," said Stanton. "Did he teach you how to carve a fluted trim?"

"Yes, sir."

"Show me." Stanton handed him a chisel and a scrap of wood.

Rob carved out the fancy trim, thinking how much he preferred this work to hoeing tobacco under Holt's forboding eye. But why spoil the day thinking about Holt? For the next fortnight he'd be doing the work that he loved. Why think about anything else?

In Stanton's home Rob found it easy enough to think only of the present—at least, most of the time. At night he dreamed of Hunter's Toyle, and when he woke up, visions of Holt and Hades and endless tobacco fields filled his mind. Sometimes he dreamed that Mattoume was in danger. Once he even dreamed she was dead; that was the worst night of all.

His waking hours, however, were pleasant ones. He met Stanton's bondservant, John Wilkins, a good-natured man who did not seem to mind that Rob had more skill than he did. Under Stanton's guidance they made good progress on Sir Lionel Biggsby's cupboard. Most of their time, however, was spent on plainer tasks: building simple chests and chairs and stools. Stanton also taught Rob something of the cooper's trade, for Virginians were always in need of casks and barrels to carry their tobacco back to England. He also showed Rob how to paddle a canoe.

Nell often came by the shop to visit, always with

the Edgehill boys in tow. Her visits weren't long—Mistress Edgehill didn't allow Nell many free moments—but during them she talked up a storm, telling Rob about all the goings-on in Parr's Hundred.

Rob had other visitors, too. Shy Kate became his friend after he made a chair out of twigs for her poppet, and Daniel followed him about like a puppy from the very first day. At first Rob wasn't sure what to do with him. But Daniel soon made it clear what he wanted: "Up!" After that, whenever Rob had a free moment, he'd set Daniel on his shoulders and take him for a ride around the house.

"I've not heard Daniel laugh like that since his parents died," Stanton said one rainy morning when he and Rob were alone in the shop, making a new table for a neighbor.

Rob was puzzled. "His parents, sir? I took him for your own."

"No," said Stanton. "He and Kate are brother and sister. Their parents died last summer, of the same sickness that took our own son."

Rob had not known that the Stantons had ever lost a child. "I'm sorry, sir."

Stanton picked up a hammer. "It was a hard time."

Rob couldn't let the subject go. "Daniel's parents—they were kin to you?"

"None whatsoever."

"But you took their children in—"

"Someone had to, lad. And we were glad to do it." Stanton went to work with the hammer, joining the top of the new table to its base with wooden pegs.

Rob stared at the sawdusty floor. The Stantons were good people, no doubt about it. But the longer he stayed in their house, the more he worried about all they did for others. They were comfortably off, but they certainly weren't rich, and yet needy folks were always knocking on their door. A leaky roof, a sickly newborn, an empty larder—whatever the trouble, the Stantons did their best to help.

Rob thought of his father. He, too, had been so kindhearted, he could never turn down a body in trouble. And yet there had been nothing to show for his kindness after he'd gone. The very people he'd helped had turned their backs on Rob. He could have starved in the gutter for all anyone cared.

Stanton set down his hammer. "What is it, lad? Something is troubling you, that much is plain."

"You're too kindhearted!" Rob knew it was not right to speak so boldly to one in authority, but he did not care. Stanton had to be warned. "If you don't watch out, some rogue is sure to take advantage of you."

Stanton chuckled. "And who would these rogues be, exactly? Daniel? Kate?"

The man wasn't taking him seriously. "I'm talking about Captain Holt," Rob said with dignity, "and men o' that sort."

Stanton sobered. "I'm sorry, lad. 'Twas wrong to tease you. Your master does indeed have a sorry reputation, though you would do well not to remark on it too loudly. Virginians don't take kindly to servants who speak ill of their masters."

Stanton's eyes were sympathetic, but nevertheless Rob looked away. "Yes, sir."

"But leaving your master out of it," Stanton continued, "it is true, what you say: There are many in Virginia—aye, and in England, too—who care nothing for the suffering of others so long as they themselves profit by it. And it is well to be on guard against them. But as to my being too kind . . ." Stanton shook his head. "'Twould be a powerful cruel world, lad, if we cared for no one but ourselves."

Rob frowned. *The world's* already *a cruel place,* he thought. *That's why a body has to look out for hisself. That's why you can't afford to be too kind.*

It seemed it was no use explaining that to Stanton, though.

"There, now." Stanton set down his hammer and stepped back from the table. "That's a job well done. Come help me with the benches, lad."

Rob nodded obediently. "Yes, sir."

For the rest of the afternoon they spoke only of carpentry.

All too quickly Rob's stay with the Stantons was over. Early in the morning on the fourteenth day they all gathered round to say goodbye. In her cradle baby Bess gurgled and cooed. John Wilkins clapped Rob heartily on the back. Kate was too shy to do more than wave at him from behind Mistress Stanton's skirts, but Daniel grabbed hold of his leg and shouted, "Lob!" which made them all laugh. For all Daniel worshiped the ground Rob walked on, he hadn't yet managed to say his hero's name correctly.

Rob pried the small boy loose and chucked him under the chin. "Be good, you rascal." He handed the boy to Mistress Stanton, who in turn handed him his much-worn jerkin, which she had mended during his stay. Then—to Rob's embarrassment—she kissed him on the cheek.

"We will miss you," she said. Rob's throat grew tight.

"Come, lad," said Stanton, handing him a paddle for the canoe. "We must be on our way. I told Captain Holt we would meet him in Jamestown at noon."

After one last round of goodbyes, Rob followed Stanton down the path that led to the palisade gate. As they passed by the Edgehills' house, Rob looked to see if Nell was about; he'd hoped to see her one last time before he left. But there was no sign of her, or of anyone else, except the smoke from the smithy fire.

Mistress Edgehill must be gadding about the village, Rob thought. *Or mayhap she's gone with Nell and her chicks to gather wood for the fire.* He turned away, disappointed.

He and Stanton were nearly at the gate when he heard Nell calling his name.

"Rob!" She was running toward him, for once without the Edgehill boys bringing up the rear. When she reached him, her face was red and worried. "Mistress Edgehill needed me to help take the cow out to pasture," she said, panting hard. "I thought I'd never get away in time to see you off. I told her you were my oldest friend, but—"

"Never mind," he said. "You're here now."

She nodded and hugged him. "Oh, Rob! I hate to see you go."

He was dismayed to notice that she was in tears. Even more disconcerting was the fact that his own eyes were feeling strangely hot and grainy. He didn't trust himself to speak.

"Courage, lass," said Stanton. "For aught we know, Rob will come again to us, by and by."

Nell turned to him, her tearful face brightening. "You mean Captain Holt might hire him out again?"

"Mayhap," said Stanton. "We can but see. In the meantime, wish us a good journey, for we must be going now."

As Nell trotted off back to the Edgehills, Rob and Stanton headed down toward the landing. When they reached the riverbank, they righted the canoe, walked it into the river, and climbed aboard.

As they paddled away from Parr's Hundred, Rob refused to turn and look behind him. Though Stanton had spoken boldly of his return, he knew he would not be coming back. Indeed, he'd likely never see Nell or the Stantons again, for once he ran away with Mattoume, all his links to Parr's Hundred would be broken. The thought left him feeling hollow inside.

But what alternative did he have? It wasn't as if a place with the Stantons was his for the asking. If he didn't run away—if he stayed in Hunter's Toyle—the most he could hope for was that Holt would hire him out to Stanton for a few weeks a year.

Was that enough to keep him from running away?

Rob looked across the river. He thought of the snarling mastiff; the muddy, snake-infested fields; the masters who had killed off six servants.

I can't bear it, he thought. *Not for the sake o' a few weeks at the Stantons'. Not when I knows there's hardly no chance of me ending up as a free man and a carpenter. Not with Holt driving me the way he does.*

Mattoume was right. He needed to run away. Run away—and never look back.

Chapter 16

That morning the crossing was both rough and quick. Rob and Stanton reached Jamestown well before the appointed hour.

Stanton led Rob to one of the houses along the town's back street, a house with a fine garden and neat wattle fence. "Wait here, lad, while I have a word with my friend Master Pryor."

Standing in the garden, Rob could see past the houses opposite to where the James River ran sparkling in the sunlight. He stared at it for quite a while, then turned his back on it and gazed at the dark forest beyond Jamestown—the forest that stood between him and Hunter's Toyle. After two weeks away from the place, it was harder than ever to face going back there.

He heard Stanton coming out of Pryor's house behind him. "Good day! And many thanks for the news."

As Rob turned, he saw Stanton hurrying toward him with a pleased expression on his face. "Good tidings, lad—but come, we must first prepare to meet with your master."

"Yes, sir." Although Rob dreaded seeing Holt again, he knew it wasn't his place to say so. He and Stanton walked to the far end of the street. When they reached the agreed-upon meeting place, Stanton said, "I've decided to make an offer for you, lad."

Rob wasn't sure he had heard right. "An offer?"

"I want to buy your indenture."

Rob's heart skipped a beat. "But Master Naylor said it was dangerous to come between Holt and his servants."

"Aye," Stanton agreed, "but in this case I'm willing to risk it. You're a good lad and a skilled one, and Holt himself brought you to my notice. So he should not be overly surprised if I make an offer for you. And there's a chance he will not be averse to it. Master Pryor says he has been caught gambling and cannot pay the fine. And he has other debts as well, which will come due at the end of the season. If he's in need of money, he's more likely to see his way to selling you."

Or mayhap he'll knock us both to the ground, Rob thought. With a temper like Holt's, there was no telling what could happen. *It would be a terrible thing, if Stanton got hurt trying to help me.*

Stanton frowned. "You don't look pleased, lad. Do you not wish to be my apprentice?"

"I never wanted nothing more," Rob said. "But Captain Holt, he's a hard man—" He stopped. Holt was coming toward them, his armored chest glinting in the sun.

"You leave your master to me," Stanton said. He stepped forward and waved his hand in greeting. "Good day, Captain Holt!"

Never one to waste time on pleasantries, Holt grabbed Rob's shoulder and asked, "Did you get your money's worth from the boy?"

"That I did," said Stanton. "Indeed, so well did the lad suit me that I should like to make him my apprentice."

Holt yanked Rob back so hard, he nearly yelped. "The boy's not for sale."

"I assure you I would pay a very fair price."

Holt kept a firm hold on Rob. "A fair price? The boy is worth a fortune to me. I need him to bring in the harvest."

"Mayhap I could buy his indenture after the harvest is over," Stanton suggested. "That would save you the expense of feeding him through the winter."

Holt shrugged. "Winter is a long way off. There's little use talking about it now."

Stanton said nothing.

Rob's heart fell.

"Of course," Holt said slowly, "if the offer were high enough, I might change my mind."

Now the bargaining began in earnest. Rob's heart pounded as Holt and Stanton hammered out terms. The sale would take place four months from now, after the tobacco was harvested. Holt would receive a twentieth of the price in advance. And what price would that be? Rob listened to the bidding, so tense he hardly noticed Holt's hand clamped around his shoulder, tight as a vise.

Stanton opened with an offer of ten pounds sterling, to be paid in good tobacco leaf. Holt laughed in his face and demanded three times that amount. Stanton went to twelve pounds, then fifteen. Holt did not budge. Thirty pounds, he said, or there would be no sale.

To Rob's dismay, Stanton shook his head and said, "Then I'll have to look for some other boy." He touched his hand to his felt hat. "Good day, Captain Holt." He stepped away without so much as a fare-thee-well to Rob.

Holt let him go a good way down Back Street before calling out to him, "Master Stanton!"

Stanton turned around.

"Mayhap I was too hasty," said Holt.

It took them another half-hour to agree on a price. Afterward they went to Master Pryor's dwelling, to have their agreement properly written out and witnessed.

While Holt spoke with Master Pryor, Rob edged toward Stanton. "You're paying more'n I am worth," he whispered, "as much as a man would bring."

"You'll be a man soon enough," Stanton said. "And you'll be a great help to me in the meantime."

At last everything was settled. Holt clearly thought he'd gotten the better of the deal, but Stanton was smiling in quiet pleasure, and Rob himself was ready to shout for joy. Once Holt's tobacco was harvested, he would be Stanton's apprentice. He would live in Parr's Hundred. He would—

"Don't stand there gaping, boy," snapped Holt. "You're my servant for another four months. And I'll not be cheated of a single hour, you can be sure of that." He shoved Rob forward. "'Tis high time we were back at Hunter's Toyle."

Even the mention of Hunter's Toyle could not dampen Rob's joy. *Four more months,* Rob told himself as Holt marched him out of Master Pryor's house. *Four more months and you'll be free of Holt forever. You'll be free of Fanshawe. You'll be free of Hades.*

And then he remembered Mattoume. His fellow servant. His friend. In the excitement of the bidding and sale, he'd forgotten all about her.

We go together, she had said. And he had agreed.

What was he going to say to her now?

Chapter 17

When Rob and Holt reached Hunter's Toyle, they found Fanshawe and Mattoume out working in the fields. As Holt told his cousin about the bargain he had struck with Stanton, Rob stood quietly by. When no one was looking, he glanced at Mattoume, who was still busy weeding. Was she close enough to hear what Holt was saying?

"We'll have the boy for the rest of the season," Holt finished. "After that we'll buy a man to replace him."

Fanshawe looked at Rob. "Stanton has already paid for him?"

"Only a small amount, to seal the bargain—enough for me to make good on our fines and buy us some shot and powder." Holt turned to Rob. "Go fetch our hoes from the house, boy. And don't take all day."

This here place looks more forsaken than ever, Rob thought as he ran toward the rickety palisade. Slowing down as he passed the broken-down gate, he skirted the growling Hades and entered Holt's hovel. When his eyes adjusted to the light, he saw Holt's long hoe leaning against the wall next to his own short one. He carried them out to the field, where Holt was waiting for him.

"Get to work, boy." Holt glared at his cousin, who was hoeing halfheartedly in the row ahead. "And the same goes for you, too, Fanshawe."

"I've been out here for hours already," Fanshawe complained, "while you've been gallivanting off to Jamestown—"

"Gallivanting?" Holt raised his hoe and thrust it into the dirt. "I do more in an hour than you do in a day, you laggard."

As the two cousins continued to bicker, Rob set to work in the row next to Mattoume. Following her silent lead, he moved steadily down the field until they were out of earshot of Holt and Fanshawe. Half hidden by the flourishing tobacco, she whispered, "We go soon, before they take you away."

So she *had* heard what Holt had said. And now he must answer her.

Rob bent his head and stared blindly at the weeds on the end of his hoe. All the way back from Jamestown he had been dreading this moment.

How could he give up the chance Stanton was offering him? How could he bear to run away, knowing he would never see Nell and the Stantons again?

From now on I looks after meself. That's what he'd said, wasn't it? Yet how could he betray Mattoume? She was the truest friend he'd ever had—and if he didn't run away with her, she'd be Holt's slave for life.

Mayhap he could help her run away on her own, he thought desperately. But that wasn't what he had promised, was it? *We go together*—that's what he'd said. And the only way he could be sure she made it safely back to her family was if he went with her. Rob's head whirled. Was he going to honor his promise? Or was he going to put himself first?

Still not sure of the answer, he raised his head and looked straight into Mattoume's eyes. And that was when he realized he couldn't turn his back on her. Not after all she'd done for him. Not when he knew it meant that she might never be free. Not when it meant leaving her to die a slave at Hunter's Toyle.

What was it Stanton had said? *'Twould be a powerful cruel world, lad, if we cared for no one but ourselves.*

Still looking straight at Mattoume, Rob said, "Yes, we go soon." And then he bent to work again, for Holt had broken off his argument with Fanshawe and was coming down the row behind him.

That afternoon Rob and Mattoume had no further chance to speak with each other, for Holt worked them hard, and he and Fanshawe were never far away. Even after supper, when Rob and Mattoume retreated to their loft, it was too dangerous to talk. Holt and Fanshawe were hardly speaking to each other, but neither one had yet gone to bed.

Though the moon was bright that night, the windowless hut, as always, was dark, except by the open door, where the moonlight shone through. Peering over the edge of the loft, Rob could barely see the two cousins in the shadows below. Only their pipes were brightly lit, as they both puffed away in the darkness.

When Holt finally spoke, his voice was like gravel. "There was a letter for you in Jamestown, cousin."

"A letter?"

"From Miss Rawlings." A paper crackled. "Here it is."

"Why didn't you give this to me when you first arrived?" Fanshawe demanded.

Holt shrugged. "I had more important matters on my mind than your love letters."

A chair scraped against the floor. "I need a candle," Fanshawe said.

"Not for Miss Rawlings's letter, you don't," Holt told him. "We've only one candle left, and I won't waste it on such trifles. If you can't wait till morning, then go outside. I warrant the moon is bright enough to read by."

Fanshawe stood still for a moment. "Very well, then, I'll read it outside." The letter crackled again as he went out the door.

A minute went by. Then Holt bellowed, "So what does she say?"

When no answer came, Holt rose and followed his cousin outside. Soon Rob and Mattoume heard them quarreling, though they couldn't make out the words.

"We talk now," Mattoume whispered. "You tell me what happen when you are away."

Rob couldn't bear to speak of Parr's Hundred, not when he knew he would never go there again. "There's nothing to tell."

"Is something," Mattoume insisted.

"What do you mean?" he said, confused.

"When we talk in field, your face—" She stopped, then began again. "What happen?"

She wouldn't be put off. He had to tell her something. So he told her about Nell.

"You find Nell?" Mattoume was startled. "Where?"

"Across the river."

"She is safe?"

"Yes."

Somehow after that it was hard to stop talking. He

found himself describing Stanton, and the carpentry shop, and Daniel, and all the people who had been good to him in Parr's Hundred.

When he finished, Mattoume was silent for a moment. Then she said, "This man Stanton buy you?"

"Yes."

"You want to go with him," she said.

It was not a question, but he answered it anyway. "Yes." There was no way he could hide the truth, not after all he'd just told her. "But I'll not go back on me word. I said I would run with you, and that's what I'm a-going to do."

"No," she whispered.

He turned to look at her, but in the darkness he could see only her outline, not her face. "What do you mean?"

"You stay," she said softly. "You be carpenter. You be with Nell. You stay."

Was she turning his offer down? "But what about you?"

"I go alone."

"But you can't," he protested. "You're only twelve. You'll never—"

"Is better alone," she insisted. "Is less worry."

"Less worry?"

"I know woods," she said. "I not get lost. If you come, is hard. You make noise. You eat wrong plants.

You need me always beside you." She paused, then said again, "Is better alone."

Rob was stunned. Perhaps there was some sense in what Mattoume was saying, but it hurt to have her talk as though he were a helpless child. "If I'm such a burden, why did you want me along in the first place? Why didn't you run that day when I fell ill, when you had the chance?"

"We friends," Mattoume said. "I not leave you."

She spoke as if the answer were obvious. But it hadn't been, not to Rob. It had never crossed his mind that he might be a hindrance to Mattoume— and that she would want him to go with her anyway. How often did you find a friend like that?

"But is different now," Mattoume continued. "Is good you stay. Is good I go."

Rob nodded slowly. Not for the first time that day, his world had turned upside down, but this time it felt as if everything were coming out right.

But what about Mattoume? She still needed to escape—and for that, if for nothing else, she needed his help. "Whatever it takes to get you safe out of here, I'll do it," he promised.

To his consternation, Mattoume didn't immediately accept his offer. "Holt flog you," she reminded him.

As if he needed reminding! *A soldier's flogging, boy.*

You'd be lucky to survive it. That's what Holt had threatened.

But maybe it wouldn't come to that. Trying to sound confident, Rob said, "Mayhap he'll think better of it and leave me alone. After all, I'm no good to him if I can't work." And then another idea came to him. "What if we make it look like you attacked me and then ran? That way Holt might not blame me at all. Leastways not enough to flog me."

Mattoume considered this. "Tricky Indian attack English boy?" In the dim loft she stifled a laugh. "Yes. Holt believe that."

"I hope so. Best we wait till he's away in Jamestown, though. Fanshawe is easier to fool."

"Yes," Mattoume agreed. Then she stiffened beside him. "They come," she warned softly. They both went still as Holt and Fanshawe came in the door.

"Do you not understand, Holt?" Fanshawe cried. "She has left me, I tell you! She has married another."

"'Tis no great loss," Holt muttered.

"I should never have listened to you," Fanshawe moaned. "I should never have left England!"

"Spare me your woes, cousin. I've heard quite enough already."

"Well, I've had enough, too. Enough of this place—and enough of you! I'm taking the first ship back to England."

From his vantage point up in the loft Rob saw Fanshawe step toward the moonlit doorway.

"God's blood, Fanshawe, but you are a fool," Holt said, his voice full of contempt. "Go back to England now and you will be a pauper. You'll not even have the money to pay your passage."

Fanshawe stopped in the doorway. "Surely you would not begrudge me that . . ."

Holt said nothing.

". . . would you?" Fanshawe finished weakly.

Holt's voice was hard as iron. "We haven't a penny to spare."

Silhouetted in the moonlight, Fanshawe slumped against the doorframe. All the fight had gone out of him. "Then I suppose I must stay," he whispered.

Holt gave a satisfied grunt. "I thought you'd see it my way. Now let's get to bed. I want us out in those fields at dawn."

Four more months, Rob told himself. *Four more months and I'll be gone forever from this place. And so will Mattoume.*

If all went well.

Chapter 18

The days came and went, and Holt did not leave Hunter's Toyle once. Rob and Mattoume began to worry that he never would, at least not until fall—and it was summer's dense greenery that would provide Mattoume's best chance for escape.

Rob had another reason to worry, one he kept secret from Mattoume. When he'd offered to help her escape, he'd been safely tucked away in the loft; it had been easy enough to be brave then. But in cold daylight, under Holt's cruel eye, courage was harder to come by.

Rob still meant to keep his promise. But every time Holt shoved him or cuffed him, a little more of his courage seeped away. Though he tried hard not to think about floggings, his nightmares were full of them. Day by day he was growing more nervous.

"What ails you, boy?" Holt demanded at dinner one day. "You're not suffering from fever, are you?"

"I—I'm fine, sir. Only tired."

Holt cuffed him. "You'll be a lot more tired when the day is done."

And Rob was. But that didn't stop the nightmares.

"'Tis a fine day," Holt observed one morning in mid-August. "I believe I'll take Hades out and shoot some game for our table." He rose from the breakfast table. "I saw bear tracks by the river yesterday. A fine addition to our larder he would make, if I can find his lair."

Fanshawe shrugged. Since he'd received the letter about his sweetheart's marriage, he'd gone broody and quiet. Most days he said nothing at all.

Holt slipped his bandolier of gunpowder charges over his head and took up his musket. "While I'm gone, cousin, you can see to the lower field. It needs worming. And be sure to keep a close eye on the servants." Ever since Mattoume had moaned aloud during the fever, Holt had held her in deep suspicion. But though he tried sometimes to startle her into speaking, so far he hadn't succeeded. "The girl is a devious sort, and bears watching. As for the boy—he's the most valuable property we have."

Fanshawe nodded, briefly and without much interest.

This time it was Holt's turn to shrug. "All right, then. I'll be back around midday."

He strode out the door and shouted at Hades, who whined in response. A chain clanked, and then Holt and Hades were off. Without thinking, Rob glanced at Mattoume. She did not meet his eyes, but her cheeks were flushed. Was this their chance?

Mattoume headed for the loft. Rob guessed she was hiding their small bag of food under her skirt.

When she came down, Fanshawe didn't even bother to look at her. Listlessly, he shouldered his hoe and led them out into the fields.

The sun rose high in the sky as they did the job that Rob hated most: worming the tobacco. Nearly every plant harbored hornworms, which had to be plucked off and then crushed underfoot.

Fanshawe evidently hated the work as much as Rob did. As the hours passed, his complexion took on a greenish hue. At last he said, "A pox on this! You, boy, watch over the girl till I return." He staggered toward the paling, leaving Rob alone in the fields with Mattoume.

Mattoume stood up straight and looked at Rob. Rob stared back at her, his stomach quaking as he thought of what might happen to him once Holt discovered she was gone. *But if she's got the courage to run, I reckon I got the courage to help her.*

"Go," he said. "Go now, afore anyone comes!"

Mattoume looked at him for a long moment, as if committing him to memory. Then she said something in Pamunkey that he couldn't quite understand. Something about friends, he thought. Before he could ask her to translate, she darted toward the trees. His heart pounded in fear and exhilaration as he watched her disappear into the deep forest.

Good luck, Mattoume. And Godspeed.

Once she was completely out of his sight, he turned his attention back to the field around him. He had done all he could to help Mattoume reach her home; now he must help himself.

He took stock of his surroundings. He and Mattoume had talked over what he should do to make it look as if she had attacked him. Holt would surely know that, barehanded, Rob was more than a match for Mattoume, so they'd decided he should find a weapon to make it believable. A rock, they'd thought—but now Rob spied Fanshawe's iron hoe lying in the dirt. Even better! He need only scuffle himself up, bang his head with the hoe, and lie moaning in the field till they found him.

He picked up the hoe, wondering how best to go about raising a bump. *It's a sight harder than I reckoned it would be,* Rob thought. *But—*

A dog barked.

Rob looked up and froze. Holt was coming out of

the woods that lay opposite the route Mattoume had taken. He was only a hundred yards off now, and coming closer with every step, a brace of birds dangling from his belt. At his side was Hades, who rushed forward, teeth bared, as soon as he saw Rob.

They're back, was all Rob could think. *They're back already. And Mattoume's only just got away—*

"Hades!" Holt yelled.

The mastiff snarled at Rob, then reluctantly came to heel beside his master.

"Y-y-you're back, sir," Rob said, trying to keep the quiver out of his voice.

"I've already shot enough for our dinner." Holt glanced down at the dead birds he was carrying, then glared at Rob across the sea of tobacco. "Why are you out here alone?"

For a wild moment Rob contemplated an attack on Holt. But that was folly. A boy and a hoe were no match for a man and a dog—never mind the musket.

He must somehow use his wits, then, to buy time for Mattoume.

"Well, boy?"

What could he say?

At least Fanshawe's disappearance was easily explained. "Master Fanshawe, he said he felt all queasy-like, sir, and so he went up to the house. And—"

"And what?"

Rob thought quickly. If he'd stuck his neck out this far, he might as well stick it out a bit more. "And the girl followed after him, sir."

The lie wouldn't hold up for long, of course. Holt would know something was wrong as soon as he reached the house. But it was the best Rob could do under the circumstances, and it would give Mattoume another quarter-hour to get away.

"Felt sick, eh? Lazy beggar! I'll soon sort him out. And the girl, too." Holt stalked off toward the palisade. Hades snapped his teeth at Rob and followed.

Rob stayed in the field, feeling as limp as Holt's brace of birds. He put the hoe down, picked it up, then put it down again. He felt weaker without it, but what did that matter? He couldn't escape what was coming.

All too soon he heard the cry he'd been dreading. "Boy!"

Holt and Fanshawe came running toward him. Hades was close at their heels. Rob's heart sank. It had taken them such a very little time to figure out what had happened.

Run, Mattoume. Run!

Holt was very close to him now. "Where is she, boy?"

Rob pretended to be puzzled. "Who—?"

"The girl," Holt bellowed. "The Indian! You said

she followed my cousin up to the house, but she's not there. And he doesn't know a thing about it."

Rob stuck to his story. "But, sir, I saw her—"

"Where?" Fanshawe asked.

"She was right behind you, sir. No more than twenty paces back, as far as I could tell. I thought you knew—"

Holt grabbed Rob's shirt. "Are you lying to me, boy?"

"No, sir, I—"

"Hades!" Holt threw a scrap of something to the dog. Rob saw it flutter down—a threadbare scarf that Mattoume sometimes wore on rainy days. Hades snapped it from the air and tore it in two.

"Find her, Hades! Find her."

Under Rob's horrified gaze, the mastiff sniffed at the ground, picked up the scent, and went rushing down the field, right to the edge of the woods.

Holt shoved Rob forward. "Follow him, you bloody liar! And you, too, cousin." He strode toward the woods. "We'll bring the girl back—dead or alive."

Chapter 19

R ob joined the hunt for Mattoume. With Holt in such a killing rage, he had no choice.

And what of the flogging to come? Rob closed his mind to it—closed his mind to everything but Mattoume, who was somewhere up ahead of them.

Run, Mattoume. Run!

But how could anyone outrun Hades? The mastiff hunted for the sheer, dark joy of it, never tiring of the chase. Holt, too, showed no signs of flagging. Rob and Fanshawe floundered through the woods, trying to keep up with them.

"After her!" Holt cried. "After her!"

Rob heard Fanshawe swear softly. But all kept on until the mastiff came to a halt. A wide stream stood in his way. *Mattoume's stream*, thought Rob. Even in this dry weather it was deep enough to throw Hades off the scent. He raised his head and whined.

Fanshawe hobbled toward the stream, his gun dangling weakly from his arms. "We've lost her," he gasped.

"The Devil we have!" growled Holt. He waded through the knee-deep stream, calling to Hades as he went. "Come, Hades. Find her!" Rob and Fanshawe followed in the dog's wake. But when they reached the other bank, the mastiff wandered aimlessly, unable to pick up the trail.

"She must have kept to the water," Holt said. "We'll have to search both banks and see where she came out."

That would take time, thought Rob—time that Mattoume could use to her advantage. Hope kindled within him. Perhaps Mattoume would get away after all.

The next thing he knew, he was flying toward the water, courtesy of Holt's boot.

"You needn't look so pleased, boy!"

Rob grabbed at the hemlocks on the edge of the stream. They saved him from a dunking—but only barely. His right knee struck a rock, and his left foot splashed into the water. He lifted his head and bit back a cry. Above him loomed Hades, all slavering tongue and sharp teeth.

"Mayhap I won't flog you after all," Holt said in a soft, dead voice. "Mayhap I'll just give you to Hades."

Rob stopped breathing. But he couldn't close his

eyes, couldn't stop staring at those pointed yellow teeth.

"But not now," Holt decided. "Not till we find the girl." He called out to the dog. "Hades!"

The mastiff bounded to his side. "Find her!" Holt commanded. "Find the girl." He urged Hades along the bank. "This way."

"You go on, cousin." Looking like death, Fanshawe sagged against a tree. "I'll wait here."

"You weasel-beaked wastrel." Holt lunged toward Fanshawe and pulled him to his feet. "You're coming with me. And so is the boy, else I'll set Hades on you both."

Rob hauled himself up from the hemlocks and scrambled after them.

Judging by the way the mastiff was wandering from bush to bush, it seemed he still had not picked up the scent. Perhaps that meant Mattoume had got clean away. Rob hoped it was so. But she hadn't had much of a start. Likely she was somewhere close by.

He sized up his surroundings. The brush along the stream bank was too low and too sparse to afford many hiding places. But up ahead, not far from the stream, Rob spied a thicket—a dense, dark mat of briars and young trees where someone might well be able to hide. As he stared at it, he saw something move near its edge, shaking the briars ever so slightly.

Hades let out a howl and raced for the briars.

"We've found her!" Holt cried, and ran after Hades.

Run, Mattoume! Rob wanted to shout. But he couldn't make a sound.

Holt ran to the edge of the thicket and readied his musket. "I have you now, girl. Come out of there, or I'll shoot."

The thicket rustled, but Mattoume did not appear. Holt fired.

The thicket rippled and quivered. From its thorns emerged the largest animal Rob had ever seen.

A bear. A wild, shaggy bear with small, fierce eyes and a long, snarling mouth. For all its size, it moved as fast as a horse.

Rob turned to run for his life. Then he remembered Mattoume's warning: *English run—bear chase them. Pamunkey stay still—bear go away.* Knowing Mattoume was far wiser than he was about the ways of the Virginian wilderness, Rob forced his shaking legs to stand firm.

Holt, however, had already started to run. Before he reached the stream, the bear caught up with him and clawed his leg. Holt screamed, a sound that turned Rob's insides to pudding. Terrified, he watched Hades hurl himself at the bear. The wild creature reared back from the still-screaming Holt and faced the new attacker. Barking madly, Hades leaped up and tore at the bear's throat.

A few yards ahead of Rob, half hidden by a tree, Fanshawe raised his gun. The blast shook the clearing but left the bear unharmed. Fanshawe cursed and reached for his bandolier.

As Fanshawe reloaded his gun, Hades backed the bear into the thicket. When the bear plunged into the briars, Hades followed after it. Soon the thicket shivered in a frenzy of motion. Grunts and yelps filled the air. Then came a terrible howl, cut off almost before it began. A moment later the bear rushed out of the briars, straight toward Holt.

Fanshawe took aim again. When the shot went off, the bear changed direction. Too terrified to blink, Rob saw the immense beast rush toward him, all fur and claws and teeth.

I'll be eaten alive, he thought.

The bear stumbled and dropped to the ground.

Fanshawe reloaded his gun. "Get in front of me, boy."

Rob could not move.

Fanshawe's voice lashed out like a whip. "I said, get in front of me."

This time Rob dared not disobey.

"Go forward, boy, and see what he does."

Heart in his mouth, Rob edged toward the fallen

bear till he stood only a foot away. The animal did not move.

Fanshawe walked up and prodded one of the bear's paws. "He's dead."

Rob's heartbeat slowed. On shaky legs he followed Fanshawe across the clearing. There they knelt beside Holt and examined his leg. The bloody wound stretched from thigh to ankle and plunged deep into the calf.

Holt was no longer screaming, but his lips were bit bloodless. "Go after the girl, you fools!" he ordered, eyes glowing. "Don't let her get away!"

Fanshawe's face hardened. For the first time Rob saw a strong resemblance between the two cousins.

"No," said Fanshawe. He pulled off his shirt and began tearing it into strips.

Holt grabbed for his musket. "After her, I say! After her!"

Fanshawe knelt and tied a strip of cloth around Holt's bleeding leg. "I've had enough of this, Holt. We're going home. Do you hear me? Home."

"Do as I say!" Holt bellowed, but there was nothing he could say to change Fanshawe's mind.

Rob nearly keeled over with relief. The hunt for Mattoume had ended.

Chapter 20

Step by weary step Rob and Fanshawe dragged Holt
back to Hunter's Toyle. Most of the time, Holt lay
in a faint, but whenever he woke, he yelled that he'd
sooner die than give up the chase.

And die he nearly did. His leg turned putrid, and
he raved like a madman for nearly a week. Only after
Captain Morgan cut the leg off above the knee did his
fever ebb.

During all this time Rob fetched and carried for
Holt, changing his bandages and emptying his cham-
ber pot. It was unpleasant work, not least because
Holt's temper worsened as his health improved. Every
time he saw Rob, he shouted for him to be flogged.
Fortunately Fanshawe took no notice. Indeed, some
days he wasn't even around to hear. He traveled to
Jamestown several times, often staying the night.

"Likely he's arranging for you to be brought up before the governor and his council," Holt told Rob. "He never could bear to punish anyone himself. When we were small, he left it to me. Now he wants the council to do it."

Rob stood motionless, a slop bucket in his hands. He'd not realized the council might take an interest in his case. But if Fanshawe asked them . . .

"I wonder what they'll do to you," Holt said softly. "Just flog you? Or brand you as well? Either way you can be sure they'll add years to your indenture—and let me break my contract with Stanton. For I'm keeping you, boy. And I'll make your life a living misery, you can be sure of that."

Rob bolted out the door, but Holt's rasping laughter followed him all the way to the broken gate. He looked out over the green waves of tobacco to the dark forest beyond.

If only he had run away with Mattoume! Now he had no chance of escape, not on his own.

The next morning Fanshawe returned from Jamestown and told Holt he had arranged their passage back to England.

"To England!" Holt sat bolt upright in his bed. "Why, you whey-faced rat—"

"Be sensible," said Fanshawe sharply. "With the girl

escaped, and your leg gone, we'll never manage to harvest the tobacco and bring it to market. We'd best cut our losses now."

"I'll not go, I tell you! I'm staying here in Hunter's Toyle!"

"You can't," said Fanshawe. "I've sold our land—and the crops on it—to settle our debts."

"Sold the land?!" Holt's face was mottled with rage. "How dare you!"

"You signed the papers yourself."

Holt snorted. "What papers?"

"Over a week ago it was—"

"I was out of my mind with fever!"

Fanshawe shrugged. "You made a fair signature. The court in Jamestown was satisfied."

Holt jabbed a finger toward Rob, who was clearing away the remains of their breakfast. "And what of him? What happens to him?"

"Two days ago I sent word to Stanton that we wish to sell the boy now. Once he pays us, we'll have enough money for the passage."

Rob kept quiet, hardly able to believe his good fortune.

Holt spat on the floor. "And what if Stanton does not come?"

Fanshawe shrugged. "Then I'll sell the boy to someone else."

Rob nearly lost hold of the trencher he was scraping. Sell him to someone else?

"It would mean breaking the bargain you made," Fanshawe said, "but no doubt the council will understand the urgency. And even if they don't, by the time they find out what we've done, we'll be long gone."

Holt was staring at the cold, black hearth. "All my life I've had so little," he whispered, "and now I am left with worse than nothing. And the boy is to blame," he added, his voice growing stronger. "He should be flogged, I tell you. Flogged within an inch of his life—"

"No one will pay good money for an injured boy," Fanshawe said sharply.

Holt ignored him. "He should suffer as I have—"

"I told you before: We need the money from his sale to pay for our passage."

"He should be flogged," Holt insisted. "And if you won't do it, the council should."

"Hell's bells, Holt, but you try a man's patience! I won't flog the boy, and I won't see the council flog him, either. And that's that." Fanshawe stalked out the door.

Holt's flat eyes fixed on Rob. "Don't underestimate me, boy. I'll have my revenge. You'll see. . . ."

Rob grabbed the empty water pail and left the dwelling.

No need to worry, Rob told himself as he dipped his pail into the creek. *Holt can't do you no real harm. Leastways he can't once Stanton gets here.*

But what if Stanton were short of money this month? What if Fanshawe's message missed him?

Rob sat by the creek for a long time, thinking of all the ways in which things could go wrong. It was a long time before he returned to the paling, and when he did, he heard Holt grumbling aloud.

Was he arguing with Fanshawe? Or just talking to himself? Either way, Rob dreaded coming within range of his temper again.

A deep voice rumbled as Holt paused for breath. Rob's head shot up. It was Stanton! He ran to the hut, water slopping from the sides of his pail. As he came through the door, he heard Holt say, "He had thieving ways, right from the start—"

"I am not a thief!" Rob set down the pail and turned to Stanton. "Sir, I beg you—" He broke off. Stanton was not alone. Standing next to him was Master Pryor, who had witnessed the agreement with Holt in Jamestown. There was no sign of Fanshawe.

"'Tis all right, lad," Stanton said. "You've no reason to be alarmed." He turned to his friend. "Master Pryor, you remember Rob Brackett?"

"I do." Master Pryor frowned at Rob. "Your master

tells us that you connived at the escape of another servant, and that you deceived him in many ways."

"The boy is a liar and a thief," said Holt.

"Don't you believe him, sir," Rob begged Stanton.

Master Pryor shook his head. "These are serious charges, lad. If true, they may be a matter for the council."

All the breath seemed to leave Rob's body. "The council?"

"Yes," said Master Pryor.

Holt's lips stretched back in a long, evil grin.

Rob began to quake.

Stanton put a hand on his shoulder. "I came here to buy an apprentice, Pryor, not to see a lad put on trial."

"'Tis for your own protection," Master Pryor began, when Fanshawe came in the door. Without sparing a single glance for his cousin, he introduced himself to Stanton and Pryor.

"May I speak with you and your companion outside?" He nodded at Rob. "You too, boy."

Over Holt's protests, Fanshawe herded them out the door and led them some distance away from the house. "My apologies to you. He's been raving like that ever since his wound festered."

Master Pryor's brow wrinkled. "Raving?"

Fanshawe shook his head sadly. "My cousin fancies

that the boy is to blame for our losing the Indian. Nothing could be further from the truth, of course, but there's no persuading him otherwise. And that's not the least of it. Why"— he lowered his voice —"he even believes that I, his own cousin, am a rat!"

Pryor's brow cleared. "Mad, is he? How unfortunate."

Fanshawe heaved a heavy sigh. "Indeed, 'tis a great sadness to see my cousin's wits so addled. But there's nothing wrong with the boy, you understand. Nothing to stop the sale." Fanshawe's eyes darted to Stanton's bag. "You have the money with you?"

As Rob looked on, holding his breath, Stanton pulled a sack from his bag and handed it to Fanshawe. "Here is your payment, in coin and tobacco notes. Let Pryor be my witness that I have fulfilled my bargain with you."

Fanshawe was already counting his money.

"'Tis all there, down to the last shilling," said Stanton. To Rob he said, "If there's anything you want from here, lad, best fetch it now."

There was nothing Rob wanted so much as to be gone from Hunter's Toyle. But his woolen doublet— the same doublet Mistress Stanton had mended—was lying in the loft, and warm clothing was scarce in Virginia.

He excused himself and went into the house, scooting past Holt as fast as he could.

"He doesn't want you, does he?" Holt laughed as Rob swarmed up the ladder to the loft. "You look like a dog, boy, come back here with your tail between your legs."

Rob found the doublet, came back down the ladder, and walked to the door. "You're wrong," he told Holt. "He does want me. And I'm a-going with him."

"What?!" Holt began to curse him.

But Rob was already outside, and Fanshawe, who had finished counting his money, was eager to see the back of him. "The boy is yours, Stanton. May he serve you well." He spoke loudly, trying to drown out the sound of Holt's swearing.

"Your cousin is in a bad way." Pryor looked concerned.

"He'll be better once the boy is gone," said Fanshawe.

"Then we'd best be on our way," said Stanton briskly. "Come, lad."

"'Tis a pity to see a man brought so low," Pryor murmured as they passed through the gate.

Rob supposed Master Pryor was right, yet what he chiefly felt as they walked out of the paling was not pity, but relief. And that relief increased with every step he put between himself and Hunter's Toyle. By the time they reached Jamestown, he felt almost safe. Yet when he and Stanton said goodbye to Pryor and went to find the canoe, Rob found himself growing uneasy again. Was it just his imagination, or was Stanton unusually quiet?

As they walked to the landing, Rob told himself it was only natural that he and Stanton did not have much to say to each other. It had been a long day, and no doubt Stanton was as tired as he was. And yet the silence did not feel natural to him. It felt heavy and strained and somehow all wrong.

Liar. Thief.

In the silence, Holt's words seemed to ring ever louder. Did Stanton hear them too?

Rob glanced at Stanton as they climbed into the canoe. What would he say if Rob told him what had really happened in Hunter's Toyle?

Don't be a gudgeon, Rob told himself. Just because Stanton didn't approve of making Indian children into servants didn't mean he'd look kindly on stealing. For that, according to Holt, was what Rob had done: He'd stolen Mattoume. What if Stanton saw it that way, too?

There's no need to tell him what happened, Rob told himself. *I'd just be sticking me neck out if I did. Likely he'd twist me own words against me. You can't trust no one in this world—*

He stopped himself. The world held its share of rogues, to be sure, but it had its good folks, too. And good folks trusted each other, or should, anyhow—

the way he'd trusted Mattoume, and she'd trusted him.

They had nearly reached the landing place when Rob finally looked back over his shoulder. "Master Stanton?"

"Aye?"

Rob kept his voice low. "I'm no thief. But . . . but I did help the girl get away."

"I wondered about that" was all Stanton said. But his face eased.

They reached the shallows and climbed out of the canoe. As they dragged it ashore and stowed it beside the other Parr's Hundred craft, Rob told Stanton a little more about what had happened. "Do you think I did right?" he finished. He didn't have doubts himself, but he was afraid Stanton might.

Stanton rubbed a hand across his beard. "There's many a man who would say no," he warned. Then he smiled. "Aye, lad. I think you did right."

"You've not heard word of her, have you? About her being found, I mean?"

"No," said Stanton. "There was talk in Jamestown about a reward, but there's been no report of her. Barring any misfortune, I warrant she's with her own people now."

Rob nodded. There was no way of knowing, of course. But he wanted Stanton to be right. He looked out over the James River, to the country that stretched far beyond. *I hope you are home, Mattoume. I hope you are safe.*

"Time we were getting back," Stanton said.

Rob nodded, his eyes still on the far horizon. What a hard country this Virginia was! And yet for all its faults, he had found a place here.

He turned and set his sights on Parr's Hundred, thinking of the people there who were waiting for his safe return: Mistress Stanton. Kate and Daniel. Nell.

"Come, lad," said Stanton.

Rob picked up his paddle and started on the pathway home.

Author's Note

In 1607 a band of Englishmen established a colony in Virginia at Jamestown—the first permanent English settlement in the New World.

The settlers planned to grow rich by mining gold; they also hoped to make glass, wine, and silk. To their dismay, the mines didn't pan out, nor did most of the other industries. What saved the settlement was tobacco, a plant grown and smoked by America's native people. The "golden weed" fetched a high price in England, where smoking quickly became very fashionable.

Growing tobacco was hard work, and the settlers soon found themselves in need of more people to help with the labor. At the time slavery was uncommon in Virginia, so most settlers bought indentured servants instead. These servants, the majority of whom came from the British Isles, signed a contract—an indenture—that "bound" them to their masters for four to seven years. In exchange, they received room, board, and ship's passage to America. If they survived their indenture, their masters were required to give them freedom dues: a new suit of clothes and a supply of food. But many servants died long before then, for English Virginia was not a healthy place. The death toll was worst in the early years of the settlement, when the colony was controlled by a group of private investors called the Virginia Company. Yet diseases like typhoid fever, malaria, and scurvy were still claiming many victims when Virginia came under the authority of the king in 1624, and mortality would remain high for much of the century.

Not all indentured servants came willingly to America. Some were convicts, forced to choose between servitude and death. Some were English prisoners of war. Others were tricked into signing an indenture. Children, especially, were unlikely to have had much say in signing a contract. At the direct command of the king and his council, hundreds of orphans from London's poorhouses were sent to Virginia as indentured servants. One such house, Bridewell, was required to send as many as one hundred children a year to the colony between 1618 and 1620. Other child servants were kidnapped from the streets.

We don't know much about what happened to these children once they reached Virginia. Like other new arrivals, many must have died of fever soon after arriving, and those who survived faced a hard life. They were required to serve their masters till they reached the age of twenty-one, and they had very few rights under law. Yet some orphans probably had a better life in Virginia than they would have had back in England—especially if they possessed a skill like carpentry, which was in high demand.

When the English came to Virginia, people called the Powhatans were already living there. (The Pamunkeys were one of the many peoples within this group, as were the Accomacks.) Relations between the English and the Powhatans were never very good, but Pocahontas, the favorite daughter of the Powhatans' chief ruler, briefly succeeded in drawing the two groups more closely together. After her death in 1617 they grew apart again, and by the mid-1620s the English and the Powhatans were essentially at war with each other.

As this book relates, the English used their guns and dogs to attack Powhatans. They frequently raided Powhatan villages just before harvest, destroying their dwellings and burning their crops. The settlers hated the Powhatans so much that they generally killed any captives they took. But since they were also desperate for servants, a few of them began keeping Powhatan children as slaves. How common a practice this was in the late 1620s is a matter for debate, since very few records from that period have survived. By 1644, however, such slavery had become so frequent that the Virginian authorities, worried about Indian reprisals, passed a law against it. Even so, before the century was over, Indian slavery had become commonplace.

Pamunkeys and other descendants of the Powhatan Confederacy still live in Virginia—and elsewhere—but the Powhatan language (including the dialect spoken by the Pamunkeys) virtually disappeared in the 1700s. Some words were written down and are still known to us: *Weroance, cawcauwasough,* and *mattoume* are among them.

English plantations in early Virginia had names like Martin's Hundred, Archer's Hope, and Basse's Choice, and the imaginary communities of Hunter's Toyle and Parr's Hundred are modeled on what we know of these settlements. Jamestown was and is a real place; you can visit the site today. You can also visit the Pamunkey Indian Museum, operated by the Pamunkey Tribe. Nearby, at Jamestown Settlement, you can even see a re-creation of what life was like in Jamestown in the early 1600s and what it was like in a Powhatan village. With a little imagination you can picture how Virginia might have looked in 1627, when *Virginia Bound* takes place.

Acknowledgments

Three cheers for the staffs at the British Library, the Waltham Public Library in Massachusetts, and the Goldfarb/Farber Library at Brandeis University, who helped me obtain the articles, letters, court records, academic tomes, and archeological reports I needed to write this book. I'm also grateful to B. J. Pryor of Colonial Williamsburg, who sent me maps and other materials and answered my arcane questions about muskets, money, and sundry aspects of Virginian life. Any errors that may remain are, of course, my own.

Helen C. Rountree's three works on Powhatan history—*The Powhatan Indians of Virginia: Their Traditional Culture; Powhatan Foreign Relations, 1500–1722;* and *Pocahontas's People: The Powhatan Indians of Virginia Through Four Centuries*—were a tremendous help to me as I wrote this book. Works by Ivor Noël Hume—*Here Lies Virginia: An Archaeologist's View of Colonial Life and History; Martin's Hundred;* and *The Virginia Adventure: Roanoke to James Towne:*

An Archaeological and Historical Odyssey—were also a great resource. Wonderful, too, were the pamphlets produced by the Association for the Preservation of Virginia Antiquities.

Other books about seventeenth-century England and Virginia that were especially useful include *American Slavery, American Freedom: The Ordeal of Colonial Virginia* by Edmund S. Morgan; *Robert Cole's World: Agriculture and Society in Early Maryland* by Lois Green Carr, Russell R. Menard, and Lorena S. Walsh; and *Home Building and Woodworking in Colonial America* by C. Keith Wilbur.

I owe many thanks to the generous members of the YAWRITER and Critters lists who read parts of this manuscript in draft, especially Kristina Cliff-Evans, Shirley Hazarin, Rukhsana Khan, Amy McAuley, Ed Stanfield, and Melissa Wyatt. I was also lucky enough to have the help of Dona Vaughn, Mary Jo Fernandez, Lisa Firke, and Resa Nelson, talented writers who read the manuscript in full and gave me encouragement when I needed it most. I'm grateful as well to Pat and Bert Greenfield, Kathi Fisler, and Rona Gofstein, for cheering me on, and to Jennifer Greene, whose thoughtful editing made this a better book.

Above all, my thanks go to my parents, for their faith in me, and to David Greenfield—the best husband, friend, and reader a writer could wish for.